Dolphin Diaries™

Ben M. Baglio

Illustrations by Judith Lawton

DANCING THE SEAS

AN
APPLE
PAPERBACK

SCHOLASTIC INC.

New York Toronto London Auckland Sydney
Mexico City New Delhi Hong Kong Buenos Aires

Special thanks to Lisa Tuttle

**Thanks also to the Whale and Dolphin
Conservation Society for reviewing the
information contained in this book**

12 11 10 9   7/0

Printed in the U.S.A.   40
First Scholastic printing, October 2002

1

"Dolphins off the port bow!"

Jody McGrath was in the saloon cabin, struggling with a difficult math problem, when she heard her father shout those magic words. Excitement flooded through her. She wanted to rush up on deck, but her morning lesson wasn't over yet.

As Jody looked hopefully at Maddie, the young woman who was their teacher on board *Dolphin Dreamer,* her little brother Jimmy piped up, "Can we go see?"

1

"*May* we," Maddie corrected him. She smiled. "Have you finished your work sheet?"

Jimmy nodded eagerly, handing it over.

"Me, too," his twin brother, Sean, chimed in.

"All right, then, since you've done your work, you may go."

Even before Maddie had finished speaking, the red-headed twins slid out from behind the table and scrambled toward the hatchway.

Jody shook her head glumly when Maddie turned to her. "I've only done half the problems," she admitted.

"And you're certainly not going to be able to solve the rest if you're sitting down here wondering what you're missing!" Maddie chuckled. "Go ahead, take a break. You can finish this later."

Jody beamed and started putting away her books. "Thanks, Maddie!" she exclaimed.

"How about you, Brittany?" Maddie asked, turning to the other girl at the table.

Brittany Pierce was the captain's daughter. Unlike Jody, and everyone else on board *Dolphin Dreamer,* she hadn't wanted to come on this voyage. Occasionally, she still liked to remind them of that. "I've seen enough dolphins to last me a lifetime," she snapped, not looking up. "I'll finish my work."

"OK," Maddie said pleasantly. "I hope you don't mind if we leave you to it."

Brittany shrugged.

Jody couldn't help feeling a little sorry for Brittany. She hadn't asked to be left in her father's care while her mother went off to France. But with her temper and sulking, Brittany was her own worst enemy. And besides, how could *anyone* not be thrilled at the chance to meet real, live dolphins? Jody loved dolphins more than anything else in the world. It was her dream to become a marine biologist like her parents.

Jody hurried up on deck, where she found her mother braced against the railing with her camcorder while her dad fielded questions from the twins.

Jody's parents, Craig and Gina McGrath, were in charge of a project known as Dolphin Universe. Because of this, the whole family was traveling the world for an entire year, studying dolphins. Dr. Jefferson Taylor, another scientist, had come along as the representative of the big oil company that had sponsored the project. He was also on deck but was facing in a different direction from the others as he peered through his high-powered binoculars.

"Yes, that's definitely a red-tailed tropic bird!" he muttered to himself.

Jody smiled. Although the middle-aged scientist often seemed more interested in bird-watching than in dolphins, his careful research techniques had made him an important member of the Dolphin Universe team. Back in September, Dr. Taylor's long hours spent analyzing data had resulted in an area near Jamaica being declared off-limits for dolphin captures.

Going to stand beside her father, Jody gazed out over the side of the rapidly moving yacht. As her eyes scanned the surface of the deep blue ocean, she saw what looked like a patch of rough, foamy water. During the past eight months they'd been at sea, Jody had learned to recognize all the signs that meant dolphins were near. Raising her eyes to the brilliant blue sky, Jody spotted a flock of seabirds wheeling and circling just above the foamy patch of ocean. Where dolphins were feeding, birds also gathered, hoping to pick up a few fish for themselves. But no matter how much she stared, she couldn't see the dolphins themselves.

"Is there time for me to run down and get my binoculars?" she wondered aloud.

Her father turned to smile at her. His own binoculars were hanging from a strap around his neck. "Plenty of time. But we're catching up to them," he told her. "The wind's in our favor, so we should come alongside them soon." He paused and touched his binoculars. "You can use these, if you like — right after the boys have a turn."

She smiled back at him. "Thanks, but I'll go get my own." She'd only had them a few months — they had been a Christmas present from her parents — so they were very special to her. As she moved away, she heard Sean and Jimmy quarreling over who should go first.

While she was in her cabin, Jody also picked up her diary and a pen. She was keeping a record of all her dolphin encounters and liked to jot down details while they were fresh in her mind.

By the time Jody got back on deck, *Dolphin*

Dreamer was rapidly drawing nearer to the school of dolphins. A strong wind filled the white sails, making the elegant yacht fly through the water. Jody picked her way cautiously across the sloping deck and settled herself firmly against the railing before raising her binoculars to her eyes.

She was immediately rewarded by the sight of several dolphins leaping high out of the water. And what leaps! Jody caught her breath in amazement. Most dolphins would just rise above the water's surface and quickly dive down again in a gentle, curving arc. These were very different. They positively shot up into the air, where they twisted and twirled, making several complete rotations before splashing down again. These were the acrobats and ballerinas of the dolphin world, and Jody recognized the species at once.

"Spinner dolphins!" she cried.

"That's right," her mother confirmed. "There are at least four different varieties of spinner dolphins here in the eastern Pacific. I think these are mostly gray spinners, although your dad has spotted some white bellies among them as well."

Jody gazed, fascinated, at the sleek, athletic creatures glittering in the salt spray and sunlight. Smaller than the bottle-nosed dolphins she knew best, they were in fact one of the smallest dolphin species, as well as being the most acrobatic. They were mainly gray: dark gray on the back, with paler gray underneath. A few had creamy white bellies. Their beaks were long and slender, with black tips.

Dolphins ahoy!

At first, Jody thought there were twenty or thirty of them, but soon she decided it was more like fifty. Now she saw that there were many more dolphins in the water that weren't leaping, and she realized there must be hundreds of them.

"Wow, I've never seen so many spinners in one place," she said, awestruck.

"They're not all spinners," her father said, examining the water closely.

"They're not?" Jody was surprised. "Isn't this all one school?"

"Oh, no," said Gina. "It's several schools traveling together. There are at least as many pantropical spotted dolphins as there are spinners — and I wouldn't be surprised if there weren't a few other species mixed in among them. Not to mention the tuna."

"Oh, yes," Jody said, frowning slightly. "The yellowfin tuna that swim in shoals along with dolphins. Then the dolphins get killed when they get caught in the nets set for the fish." Thinking about such a fate for the animals she loved best in the world made Jody's stomach hurt.

Her mother was nodding. "That's right. It used to be

pretty bad — nearly eighty-five percent of the spinner population was wiped out before the 1990s. But things are much better now."

"I can't see any tuna," said Sean. He was hanging nearly upside down over the railing.

Craig grabbed hold of the waistband of Sean's shorts and hauled him back. "You can't see the fish because they stay down deep. They don't need to come up for air. Unlike the dolphins, and unlike you, my boy!" He ended sternly, "We don't want to scare away the dolphins with a man overboard!"

Jimmy made a face at Sean, who looked sheepish.

"I just wanted to have a look," he muttered. "How do the fishermen know where they are, if they can't see them?"

"In the Pacific Ocean," Craig began, "wherever there are dolphins there will also be tuna. So tuna fishermen keep an eye out for large groups of dolphins."

Maddie, who had been talking with Cameron Tucker, the young first mate, now approached the McGraths. "Sean and Jimmy, it's time for your English lesson," she said. "Let's go down below."

Sighing and shrugging, the boys wandered away.

Maddie paused before following them. "You can have another twenty minutes off," she told Jody. "Then finish those math problems, OK?"

"OK," Jody agreed. "See you later, Maddie." She turned her attention back to the huge group of dolphins, eager to see more of the spinners. Although she had encountered spinner dolphins briefly in the Caribbean, she had never been able to spend much time with them or really get to know any of them as she longed to.

She gazed through the glasses, picking out one of the most active spinners to focus on. The powerful binoculars seemed to bring her right up close to the dolphin. As it twirled its whole body around, the water cascaded from all sides in a glittering spray. Jody could almost feel it against her own face. As *Dolphin Dreamer* surged forward, the wind in Jody's hair gave her the feeling that she was soaring along through the waves, just like the graceful dolphin she was watching.

All too soon, the boat began to pull away from the dolphins. Jody gazed wistfully after them until they were only specks in the distance, wishing that her father would give the order to change course and follow the dolphins, as he sometimes did.

As if she'd read Jody's mind, her mother said, "Don't worry, this area is full of spinners. We might even see that same group again — they'll easily range more than thirty miles in one day."

Jody carefully put her binoculars into their case. "I'm going to catch up on my diary now, Mom," she said. "Could you please let me know when it's been twenty minutes?"

Gina smiled at her. "Of course, sweetheart."

Jody climbed up to her favorite spot on the forward deck and made herself comfortable before she began to write.

February 9 — midmorning — eastern Pacific Ocean
Just spotted a big, mixed group of spinner and pantropical spotted dolphins, the most I've ever seen in one place. I was reminded of the first time I ever saw spinners, in the Caribbean back in September. That was when we'd just met Luisa Suarez from the Whale and Dolphin Pro-

tection League. I remember her telling me that even though the tuna fishing industry has taken steps to stop so many dolphins being killed in their nets, many still die that way even now.

The thought of the danger posed by fishermen made Jody feel anxious. She stopped writing and looked around. There was nothing in any direction but the sea and the sky. With her binoculars, she could see a hazy cloud on the horizon ahead, but absolutely nothing else.

Luckily, there don't seem to be any fishing boats around here, so the dolphins are safe for now. We haven't seen any boats at all for a long time. In fact, we haven't seen anything or anyone for nearly four weeks! Just the endless sea and the sky. It is so strange — we could be the only people left in the whole world. I am starting to forget what it's like to live on land or ever see anyone except the people on this boat! I don't know how people managed in the olden days, sailing off into the unknown the way they did. . . .

Jody's mind drifted back. *Dolphin Dreamer* had set sail from Florida eight months ago, in June. They had traveled through the Caribbean, as far south as Venezuela, before crossing the Panama Canal into the Pacific Ocean. Christmas Day had been spent in the Panama Canal Zone — the oddest Christmas she had ever known. There hadn't been room for the usual number of gifts, but they'd all taken turns in the tiny galley to cook up a huge and exotic Christmas dinner. Two weeks later, they had crossed the equator and sailed past the Galápagos Islands. That was nearly four weeks ago.

By now, they were running low on supplies. Meals were getting rather dull, despite the most imaginative efforts of their cook, Mei Lin Zhong. Jody had given up asking when they would finally see land again. She knew that Harry and Cam were expert sailors, but the Pacific Ocean was enormous, and the islands that dotted its expanse were small and widely scattered. So much depended on the wind and the weather, it was impossible to predict their schedule exactly.

"Jody." Her mother's voice roused her from her thoughts. "Your twenty minutes are up."

"Thanks, Mom." Jody had one more good look around. Still nothing in sight but the cloud on the horizon. Maybe it would rain later. She went below to tackle the rest of her math problems.

Jody worked hard for the rest of the morning. After math, they had a history lesson. Then it was time to clear away their books and papers and transform the big table from classroom to dining area.

Lunch was rice and beans. Jimmy looked unhappy when he saw the big bowls set out. "Can't I have a sandwich instead?" he asked.

Mei Lin, the petite Chinese woman who was the boat's engineer as well as the cook, shook her head gently. "Sorry, Jimmy, but there isn't any more bread. We ran out of flour to make it three days ago."

"The beans taste pretty good if you put ketchup on them," Sean said, handing his brother the red plastic bottle.

"Not as good as fresh bread, though," Brittany said.

"Salad and fresh vegetables are what I miss," Gina said wistfully as she passed the rice bowl along.

"For me it's fresh fruit," said Maddie.

"Don't mind them, please, Mei Lin," said Dr. Taylor. "You do a wonderful job. Everything you cook tastes delicious!"

"Thank you, Dr. Taylor," Mei Lin murmured. "Luckily, we still have something to add to the rice. But if I don't get to go shopping soon, we might have to put up with plain rice."

"I hope we won't get down to that," Jody said. "I miss those great cakes and pies you used to make!"

"You're all a bunch of wimps," said Craig. He was straight-faced, but his eyes twinkled mischievously. "Thank goodness for canned food is what I say! Two hundred years ago, we'd consider ourselves lucky to be eating a couple of hard, stale biscuits full of weevils at every meal."

"Oh, yuck, Dad!" Jody protested.

Her father gazed innocently at her. "What's wrong with a nice, chewy weevil? Insects are full of useful protein."

Jody and Brittany rolled their eyes at each other.

"I'm glad you feel that way, Craig," said Gina, trying not to smile. "You'll just love the special birthday dinner Mei Lin and I have planned for you. . . ."

Craig's eyes widened with alarm and everyone laughed. "Hey, wait a minute," he protested. "I said *useful,* not delicious!"

Cam Tucker was the first to finish eating. "If you'll excuse me, I'll go take over at the helm so Harry can come down for his lunch," he said.

Jimmy pushed aside his plate. "Can I help?" he asked.

"And can I come, too?" Sean chimed in at once.

Cam grinned. "Sure," he said. "I guess I can find something for you guys to do."

Soon after Sean, Jimmy, and Cam had left, Harry Pierce came down the hatch, greeted them, and sat down at the table. He was a big man with a weather-beaten face partially covered by a thick, graying beard.

Mei Lin gave him a plate of rice and beans. "I warmed it up for you, Harry," she said. "And I added a dash of pepper sauce, just the way you like it."

Suddenly, there was a cry from outside.

"Land ho!" shouted Jimmy.

His brother's voice echoed, "Land ho!"

For a moment, everyone froze except Harry, who was hungrily digging into his meal.

"Is it true, Daddy?" Brittany broke the silence.

Harry nodded, his mouth full.

Jody jumped up from her seat and scrambled up the hatchway steps, closely followed by Brittany, Gina, and Craig.

Sure enough, there was land, dead ahead. What had seemed a few hours earlier to be a cloud on the horizon was now revealed as a lush, green, mountainous island. Jody drank in the sight. Land at last!

"That's Hiva Oa — one of the Marquesas Islands," said Cam, grinning at them. "We've made it!"

2

Everyone was on deck as Cam sailed *Dolphin Dreamer* closer to the island of Hiva Oa and into the shelter of Traitors' Bay. Nobody wanted to miss the long-awaited moment of landfall after weeks at sea.

Jody and Brittany perched on the forward deck, gazing ahead as the brilliant green mountains loomed closer. Their jagged peaks were veiled by mists, and their steep sides were thickly forested. A waterfall cascaded down into a valley like a rippling silver chain.

As they drew nearer, Jody could see thickets of coconut palms lining the rocky shore. They sailed

18

through a narrow passage that opened into a sheltered harbor with a jetty where several boats were tied.

Everyone worked together to take down the sails and stow them away, and soon *Dolphin Dreamer* was tied to the jetty with the other boats.

"The first thing we must do is register with the Gendarmerie," said Harry.

"What's the Gendarmerie?" asked Jimmy, stumbling over the word.

"That's French for police station," Maddie explained. "The Marquesas are a French colony."

"And since we're not residents, we have to check in, give our names, and say how long we plan to stay," said Harry. "You don't all have to come — I can take your passports and take care of the red tape myself."

"Where is the police station?" asked Gina, shading her eyes as she scanned the bay.

Jody had been wondering the same thing herself. She could see a lighthouse perched on a rocky point, and there was a wooden shack farther along the shore with a beat-up old truck parked next to it, but nothing that might have been a police station.

"It's in Atuona, the main town on this island," replied Harry. He pointed to the road that wound away uphill. "My guidebook says it's about a three-mile walk."

"Walk!" Gina echoed. "Hmm, I'm not sure I'm up to a three-mile hike today."

"I'll come with you, Harry," Mei Lin volunteered. "I'd like to check out the shopping." She grinned at the twins. "Before some crew members go on a hunger strike!"

February 9 — before supper — Hiva Oa
This has to be the most beautiful place in the world! And everyone is so friendly. They don't treat us like strangers. As soon as anyone sees us, they smile and say, "Bonjour!" Luckily for us, Maddie knows French, because we haven't met anyone who speaks English. She chatted to everyone we met, especially to a man on the beach who gave us some fresh coconut milk to drink — it was delicious. He had tattoos all over his arms and legs. Maddie said that tattooing was an important part of ancient Polynesian culture, and the Marquesan Islanders were especially famous for it. Some little girls came running over to

give us flowers and welcome us to their island. They gig-gled like mad when I said, "Merci," so I wonder if I'm say-ing it right.

There is so much to describe, I don't know where to start. I'll leave it for later, anyway, because dinner will be ready any second, and my mouth is watering. Mei Lin came back from town with loaves of French bread, cheese, bags of fruit, and freshly caught seafood. We are going to have a wonderful feast tonight!

The next morning, they discussed their plans for the day over breakfast. The rich scent of freshly brewed coffee filled the cabin, and Mei Lin had more surprises in store — warm croissants and fresh fruit salad.

"This is definitely my idea of paradise," said Jefferson Taylor. The scientist beamed as he divided a croissant and spread thick strawberry jam on it. "I've already spotted some interesting birds this morning. I thought I might spend a few hours bird-watching, if you don't have any objections." He turned to Craig and Gina.

"None at all," said Craig. "I think we all deserve a break. We'll be getting down to work again soon enough. Gina and I thought we'd take the kids out to explore the island. Not that I have any idea of what there is to see. . . ."

"I do," Maddie said unexpectedly.

She laughed as they all looked at her. "The Polynesian islands are kind of a passion for me," she admitted. "I've been reading about them since I was a kid. All my life I've wanted to come here and see them firsthand — the Marquesas, Tahiti, Samoa, the Cook Islands. . . . Being here is a dream come true."

"Wow, that's great, Maddie," Craig said warmly. "Would you be our guide and let us tag along?"

"I'll do my best!" Maddie laughed.

Although Jody's legs felt weak and wobbly after so many weeks without much exercise, she was eager to go exploring, especially when she heard Maddie describe the amazing tribal ruins in the jungle.

"There are huge stone structures and wonderful carved statues of Polynesian gods," Maddie explained. "I'd really like to see at least one of those sites."

"Sounds wonderful," Gina agreed, her dark eyes

sparkling. "If we're all finished eating, why don't we get started?"

Half an hour later, the McGraths, Maddie, and Brittany headed up the dusty road away from the harbor. Harry, Cam, and Mei Lin stayed behind to work on the boat, and Dr. Taylor wandered off in another direction, binoculars around his neck and bird book in hand.

"How far do we have to walk?" Brittany asked warily. They were all finding the feeling of solid ground beneath their feet hard to get used to again.

Maddie chuckled. "With any luck, not far at all! Remember that man on the beach who gave us those fresh coconuts? Well, I had a word with him, and it turns out he has a truck and makes a little extra money as a guide and taxi service for visitors. So I asked him to come back for me this morning — and I told him there might be a whole group of us!"

Right on cue, there was the rumbling sound of a motor, and a battered white pickup truck came rattling around the bend in the road.

When the driver got out, Jody recognized him from

the day before. His body art made him unmistakable. He wore a sleeveless vest and shorts that revealed elaborately patterned tattoos on his dark, smooth arms and legs. These weren't like any tattoos she'd ever seen before — they were all abstract, swirly designs in black ink.

He smiled and spoke in French to Maddie, who introduced him to everyone. "This is Namu," she said. "He's suggested we could visit an ancient temple in the jungle."

"Sounds great," agreed Craig. "I've got dibs on the backseat!"

Gina and Maddie got into the cab of the truck with Namu, and everyone else piled into the open back. Jody breathed in the warm, flower-scented breeze as the truck rattled and bounced along the road. Soon they entered the dim green shade of the jungle. The air here was moist and smelled unusually sweet and delicious.

"It smells like cookies," said Sean.

"I'll bet it's wild vanilla," Craig said. "And I can smell mint, and bananas, and . . . hmm, that smells like your mom's favorite perfume!"

Every time they passed a flowering bush, a different perfume would rise up around them. Away from the sea breezes, the air was still and humid. It was very quiet except for the rumble of the engine. As they traveled deeper into the jungle, the truck moved more slowly along the steep, rugged road.

Eventually, the road ended and they had to stop. Namu explained they would have to go on foot from there.

"He says that the jungle is full of footpaths that have been used for centuries," Maddie explained. "Long ago, a different tribe of people lived in each isolated valley."

They followed him along a narrow path, deeper into the jungle. Sunlight filtered dimly through the trees overhead. Jody thought of the rain forest she had visited in Venezuela. This was a very different type of forest. Although just as lush, it was lighter, airier, and cooler. Even amid the many scents of green and flowering plants, Jody could still pick out the faint, salty tang of the sea. She spotted a few birds moving overhead, but there was a lot less wildlife on this remote Pacific island than in the South American forest.

Suddenly, Namu stopped. He was gesturing and pointing as he spoke in French. Maddie translated: "He says this temple was built by his ancestors many hundreds of years ago."

What temple? Jody wondered. Then, as she peered in more closely, she saw a large block of black stone overgrown with vines. Going closer, she saw that it was a fallen wall.

Then she saw other slabs of carved stone and realized that they were standing inside what must once have been a massive building. As she looked more closely, she could see pictures that had been carved into the rock. She recognized a fish and a turtle, and then there were patterns like the ones tattooed on Namu's arms.

"Ooh, look!" exclaimed Brittany, tapping Jody on the arm.

Jody turned and caught her breath in alarm as she noticed a fat little man crouching in the bushes, staring at her. Then she relaxed. It was only a statue.

"That's a tiki," Maddie explained, coming up behind her. "You find them all over the Polynesian islands.

Following the jungle path with Namu . . .

They come in all sizes and can be carved from stone, like this one, or wood."

As Jody gazed around her, she saw there were lots more tikis hiding in the foliage at the edge of the path. Most of them were fat and rather ugly, with crudely carved features. Some were smaller than the twins, while others were taller than her father.

"This must have been an amazing place," Gina commented.

"I think it still is," Craig said softly, gazing around at the half-hidden ruins, and everyone agreed.

February 10 — evening — Hiva Oa
Maddie says that the Marquesas Islands are full of ancient ruins like the ones we saw today and that almost none have been excavated. There is so much to be discovered here. . . . I can't wait to do some more exploring! Also, Mom has promised we can do some diving — she says there are lots of good dive sites in the Marquesas. I hope we find one that the dolphins like, because, as wonderful as the land is, it is the local dolphins that I most want to discover!

When Jody woke the next morning, she knew something was different, but at first she couldn't figure out what it was.

She was in her own familiar bunk. Morning light filled the cabin. She could hear the sounds of Brittany breathing in her bunk and the gentle slap of waves against the hull. She felt the familiar sensation of movement as *Dolphin Dreamer* glided along under sail. . . .

Wait a minute. Sailing? Jody sat up abruptly. They should still be tied to the jetty in Traitors' Bay! She was sure their schedule made time for them to spend at least a week in the Marquesas. . . .

Jody dressed quickly in shorts and a T-shirt and hurried up on deck to find out what was going on.

She found Harry alone at the helm.

"Good morning," he greeted her. "You're up early, Jody!"

Jody gazed out at the island of Hiva Oa, its green peaks already receding into the distance. "I didn't know we were going to leave so soon," she said sadly. "There was so much I wanted to do. . . ."

"Not ready for another long spell at sea, eh?" Harry

chuckled. "Don't worry! We'll reach Nuku Hiva in a few hours."

"How long are we going to stay there?" Jody asked cautiously.

"At least a week. There's a French scientist based there who's studying dolphins. Your parents are anxious to meet him and learn all about his work," Harry explained.

Jody grinned. She was relieved and excited to hear that they hadn't seen the last of the Marquesas Islands.

February 11 — after lunch — somewhere near Nuku Hiva We've just come alongside another big, mixed group of dolphins — spinners and spotted — maybe even the same group we saw a few days ago. I have been watching one especially acrobatic spinner and wondering if it isn't the same one I noticed before. Unfortunately, compared to animals like cats or horses, all the dolphins of a particular species look very much alike. Unless you really study them closely or know them really well, it can be nearly impossible to tell them apart.

Jody looked up to use her binoculars again. *Dolphin Dreamer,* gliding along at top speed with its sails full of the strong and steady wind, was just overtaking the slower dolphins. Or so it seemed. Just then, as Jody watched, about a dozen of the spinners split away from the main group and came bounding through the waves directly toward the sailboat. Then they swam along-side the boat, surfing along on the bow-wave in front.

This behavior was called bow-riding, and nearly all species of dolphins seemed to enjoy it. Sometimes dolphins even rode the waves created by the move-ment of large whales! Jody always loved it when wild dolphins hitched a ride with them. Calling out to alert her parents, she leaned over the side to watch.

The sleek, gray spinner dolphins were jostling and butting one another as they competed for the best po-sition at the crest of the wave. Jody grinned happily as she listened to their excited squeals and the rapid chat-tering noises they made. Leaning out over the side, with the wind in her hair and the salt spray on her face, she could almost imagine she was one of them, half swimming, half flying.

She studied the especially acrobatic dolphin as it came alongside the boat. It was slightly bigger than the others and appeared to be the fastest and the strongest. It managed to make its way to the very front of the boat and held that position, knocking the others aside easily with a flick of its tail or a powerful flex of its smooth, streamlined body. Each time it defeated a rival, it let out a stream of chattering squeaks, as if to say, "How dare you!"

Eventually, the others gave up. Unchallenged, the lead dolphin now began to make higher spinning leaps out of the water.

As she watched, Jody counted under her breath. "One . . . two . . . three . . . four . . . five!"

After five full-body rotations, the spinner sank back beneath the water again. When it surfaced again, Jody had her binoculars ready. The magnification made the dolphin look close enough to touch. She ran her eyes along the shining gray back. Seeing the skin up close, Jody knew this was not a young dolphin. Dolphin calves had smooth, unmarked skin. This dolphin had a number of scars that showed up as paler gray lines against the darker gray. Jody noticed one that stood out on the dorsal fin. It was a twisting, spiraling shape that made her think of Namu's tattoos.

Jody put down the binoculars and reached for her diary, wanting to make a quick sketch of the shape before she forgot. As she did, she noticed that the spinners had grown tired of their sport. One by one, they were peeling away from *Dolphin Dreamer* to return to the larger group.

The dolphin Jody had been watching was the last to go. She followed it with her eyes, wondering if she would see it again. If she did, she was determined that she would recognize it.

Jody went back down to the lower deck where her parents were gazing out to sea. She noticed that her mother had the camcorder. "Did you get those bow-riding spinners?" she asked.

"Sure did, honey," replied Gina, smiling. "Thanks for the heads-up!"

"Looks like we're not the only ones who've found some dolphins today," Craig commented. He was looking through his binoculars.

"What do you mean?" Jody asked.

"See that tuna boat over there?"

Her stomach clenched with anxiety, Jody raised her own binoculars and spotted the boat he meant. As she watched, she saw two smaller boats speeding away from the bigger boat.

"What's happening?" she asked.

"They'll use the speedboats to chase after the dolphins, then round them up and herd them toward the big boat," explained Craig.

"Like dogs herding sheep," said Gina. "But it isn't as cruel as it looks. They won't hurt them, Jody," she added.

"They're rounding them up because the tuna will follow the dolphins," Jody said slowly, reasoning it out. "And then they'll throw a net around them all."

"That's right," Craig agreed. "But remember, dolphins come up to the surface to breathe — tuna don't. The idea is that the net closes well below the surface, trapping the tuna, which can then be winched up on board, but letting the dolphins at the top swim away."

"But what about dolphins that are diving, that don't

come to the surface like the fishermen expect?" she asked. "They might panic or just get tangled up."

"Well, if the fisherman is 'dolphin-friendly,' he'll have safety panels to let the dolphins escape," Gina said. "He can hire divers to help herd the dolphins toward those panels. Also, these days nets are made in a way that dolphins are less likely to get tangled up in them, and the fishermen dip them much deeper."

Jody gazed out at the tuna boat. They were sailing closer to it now. "How can we find out if that's a dolphin-friendly boat or not?" she wondered.

"Use your binoculars again," suggested her father. "Check the flag. Quite a few countries — including the United States — have agreed to follow more dolphin-friendly fishing procedures."

Jody turned her binoculars on the boat and focused them until she was able to read the name. "It's called *Zelda,*" she said. "And its flag . . ." Raising the glasses, she brought the briskly waving flag into view. She began to smile at the familiar sight of the American Stars and Stripes. "It's one of us!" Jody cried happily.

* * *

From a distance, Nuku Hiva looked like another beautiful, green, mountainous island. But Taiohae Harbor, where they landed, was much bigger and busier than their anchorage on Hiva Oa. It was clear from the traffic that Taiohae, although small, was a bustling modern town by comparison.

As they motored slowly toward the wharf, looking for a place to tie up among other boats of all sizes, Harry said, "This isn't quite the paradise I'd expected."

Looking down at the muddy brown water, Jody had to agree. She had been looking forward to swimming — but not in this dirty water. The sea was rough, too, and the choppy waves made *Dolphin Dreamer* pitch from side to side in a most unpleasant way.

Already, Brittany was looking rather green. "I feel sick," she muttered.

"Me, too," said Gina. She looked at Harry. "I don't suppose there's anywhere else we could anchor? Somewhere more peaceful?"

Harry glanced at the sky. "We've got plenty of time before sundown," he said thoughtfully. "Trouble is, I've never sailed around here before, so I don't know where to start looking."

"I'll go below and check the charts," Cam offered.

"What about Anaho Bay?" said Maddie.

Harry and Cam looked at her with surprise.

"Maddie is a treasure trove of knowledge about this part of the world," said Craig with a grin.

Maddie smiled and ducked her head shyly. "Anaho Bay is where Robert Louis Stevenson anchored his yacht while he was visiting the Marquesas," she explained. "The descriptions of it are magical."

"Robert Louis Stevenson," Sean repeated. Then his eyes widened. "Hey, didn't he write *Treasure Island?*"

"That's right," said Maddie.

"Wow," Jimmy exclaimed. "Maybe *this* is the treasure island!"

"I don't know about that." Harry chuckled. "But if Anaho Bay was good enough for Robert Louis Stevenson, I think it's good enough for me!" He nodded at Cam. "Get ready to cast off."

"Anaho Bay, here we come!" called Craig as he helped Cam let out the sails again.

3

The coastline of Nuku Hiva was rocky with many sheer cliff faces where no boat could land. But there were also narrow inlets that led to hidden, sheltered bays. Anaho Bay was one of these. Cam found it on the chart, and Harry set a new course.

Jody perched up on the forward deck, where she enjoyed the cool breeze and the feeling of speed as the sleek, oceangoing yacht flew along. She was the first to notice the dolphins that joined them.

"Hey, we've got company!" she called excitedly to her parents.

The lead dolphin looked familiar. Grabbing her binoculars, Jody focused them on that one. It was a tricky business, trying to zero in on the moving dorsal fin of a leaping dolphin, but she managed it and was rewarded by a glimpse of the distinctive spiral marking she had noticed before. She broke into a delighted smile.

"They've come back!" she cried. "That's the same dolphin!"

"Are you sure?" asked Gina, coming up and putting her hand on Jody's shoulder.

"Absolutely sure," Jody said. She explained about the scar she had noticed.

"I guess that tuna boat didn't manage to catch them, then," said Gina thoughtfully. "Otherwise, they'd never have gotten here so quickly."

"Maybe they weren't going back to the bigger group like we thought," said Craig, gazing over the side at the leaping bow-riders. "They might have been heading somewhere else. Or it could just be that the one you recognize, Jody, has joined up with a different group. Spinners will often move around from group to group, sometimes as much as several times in the same day. They're very different from pilot whales, for example, who spend nearly all their lives with the same pod."

Jody leaned over the side, drinking in the sight of smooth, gleaming gray bodies as they rose briefly into the air and then sank down again. She counted nine of them before turning her attention back to the one with the spiral marking. It was definitely the fastest and the most agile of this group, effortlessly taking the lead once again. As it leaped out of the water and twirled, it sent a glittering spray of water in all directions. Jody felt the spray on her face and arms, and she laughed with pleasure.

She really wanted to give this particular spinner dolphin a name. "Do you think the leader is male or female?" she asked her parents.

"Definitely male," Gina replied at once. "As far as I can see, this is an all-male group."

"How can you tell?" Jody asked. She was surprised by her mother's certainty. In most dolphin species, males and females looked identical.

"Spinners are a bit different from other types of dolphins," her father explained. "Adult males develop what's called a keel — that's a bulge underneath the tail. Calves and females don't have it, but it's very noticeable in adult males. Have a look when they jump up."

Jody fixed her attention on the lead dolphin again. The next time it leaped completely out of the water, Jody looked carefully. She saw the keel immediately. Once you knew to look for it, it was impossible to miss.

Now whenever a spinner leaped clear of the water, Jody checked out its tail. She soon realized her mother was right. Every one of the nine bow-riding dolphins was male.

"They're certainly staying with us a long time," commented Gina. "I wonder what the attraction is?"

"It's got to be Jody," said Craig promptly. "They've heard about her through the worldwide dolphin web. This is the girl who makes friends with dolphins — they want to see for themselves!"

"Oh, Dad, don't be so silly!" Jody exclaimed. Her father's teasing made her feel self-conscious. She leaned farther over the side, letting the wind and the ocean spray cool her hot cheeks.

The lead dolphin made one of his highest leaps yet. His whole body rose above deck level. For a moment, Jody and the dolphin were eye to eye, only inches apart. As she gazed into his bright eye, he gazed back. She felt the deep, warm shock of connection as she

My new friend

recognized the intelligence in his gaze. Of course her dad had been teasing, yet she suddenly realized that this dolphin was curious about her, just as she was about him.

Then, as she watched him spin, she heard her mother count the rotations out loud —

"Three . . . four . . ."

The perfect name for this dolphin came into her mind.

"Five . . . six . . . seven . . ."

"Twister!" Jody cried.

"Eight!" Gina exclaimed. "Eight full spins, that's got to be a record!"

Just before Twister splashed down again, he seemed to smile at Jody. She had the feeling that he approved of his name. Then he vanished under the water.

The dolphins stayed with them all the way to Anaho Bay. As Harry steered the boat around a spit of land into the clear, calm water, the bow-riders suddenly split away from the boat and shot rapidly ahead, directly into the bay.

Jody raised her binoculars to watch them go. Then she caught her breath with astonishment. "Look!" she cried. "The bay is full of dolphins!"

It was one of the most amazing sights she had ever seen. Hundreds of spinner dolphins were frolicking in the water. Males and females, adults and calves — all were leaping and spinning, diving and swimming. Yet the bay was big enough that there was room for hundreds more.

Dr. Taylor, Brittany, Maddie, and Mei Lin joined the others on deck to watch this astonishing show of marine acrobatics.

"What do you want me to do, Craig?" asked Harry, frowning with concentration as he tried to keep the boat on an even course. "Shall we hang back? Or go somewhere else? Will it disturb the dolphins if we enter the bay?"

"Oh, I hope not. I'd love to stay here!" Jody exclaimed impulsively. Her eyes scanned the bay, trying to pick out Twister among all the others. They

'+ leave now!

;ave her an understanding smile. "It

should be all right," he told Harry. "Can we sail in without an engine, though? This is a big bay. There's plenty of room for them to avoid us if they want to."

The dolphins didn't seem bothered as *Dolphin Dreamer* glided into the sheltered waters of the bay. The yacht was coasting gently now, no longer moving fast enough to attract bow-riders. A few of the smaller spinners swam up close, as if to check out the boat, but then quickly dived down and shot away again. None of the others seemed very interested. They were too involved in their own play.

As Cam and Harry began to haul down and stow the sails, Jody spotted Twister again. Her heart leaped as he swam back toward the boat. It was almost as if he was welcoming *Dolphin Dreamer* into this dolphin playground. He stayed nearby as he leaped and whirled in the air, as if he was putting on a special performance for Gina's camcorder.

"Your Twister is a real star!" Gina told Jody with a chuckle. "I don't think I've ever seen a spinner make quite so many complete rotations. He never seems to get tired, either!"

"He's great, isn't he?" Jody agreed happily.

"Yeah, he is pretty good," said Brittany. She had joined everyone else on deck to watch the show. Even she was entranced by the magical sight of this tropical bay filled with leaping dolphins.

As the water turned dark gold, reflecting the sunset, the spinners' activity slowed down. They began to leave the bay, swimming in small groups out to sea.

"I'd better get cooking," exclaimed Mei Lin, hurrying away.

The others began to go below as well. Only Jody remained on deck, gazing down at Twister, who was still swimming in wide, slow circles around the bay. The quiet water echoed with his high-pitched cries. Jody had the impression he was rounding up stragglers, making sure none of the younger or slower dolphins was left behind.

Finally, when it was almost dark, Twister swam back to the boat. When he was directly beneath Jody, he began to leap out of the water and spin.

". two . . . three . . . four," Jody counted softly

It seemed to be his farewell. Returning to the water, he shot away to join the other dolphins.

Jody watched him disappear and crossed her fingers as she hoped he would come back again the next day.

February 12 — after breakfast — Anaho Bay, Nuku Hiva
No sign of Twister or any other spinners in the bay this morning. Assuming that spinners are like the other dolphins I've met, they probably have a regular routine. I'm guessing they'll come back again late this afternoon. I can't wait!

Right now, the bay is quiet and peaceful, and we've got it all to ourselves. The water is so clear I can see fish swimming under the surface. This place reminds me of the Caribbean: calm, clear blue water and a white sandy beach with palm trees. I sure hope we get a chance to do some diving here. It's been ages since my last dive, and this looks like the perfect spot!

Mom and Dad need to go back to Taoihae today to try to make contact with the local dolphin researcher. His name is Dr. Olivier Serval. I'd like to meet him later and learn about his research, but today I want to hang aroun the bay. Cam volunteered to sail back to Taoihae, to give Harry a break, and Harry said that anybody who wanted to stay here with him and relax in paradise was welcome! So Sean, Jimmy, Brittany, and I are all staying. We can swim and go exploring after our morning lessons.

Jody broke off, guessing from the buzz of activity that it was time to get a move on.

On deck, close to where she was sitting, Cam and Craig were setting the sails and getting ready to take up the anchor. Harry was just finishing pumping up the inflatable dinghy they would use to go ashore.

Jody hurried down to her cabin to gather up the things she'd need for the day: bathing suit, shoes, sunblock, a book. She'd just put her diary into her backpack when her mother came in.

"Jody, sweetheart, I'm counting on you to keep an eye on your brothers today," said Gina. "Harry deserves a rest, so don't let them pester him too much, OK?"

"Sure," Jody agreed. "But isn't Maddie staying? What __ lessons?"

Her mother smiled. "I guess you're getting a day off. We need Maddie with us today. My French is awfully rusty, and I don't know about Dr. Serval's English, so we may need her to translate for us," she explained. "Mei Lin will be coming, too. She wants to check out the markets in town."

Just then, they heard Cam calling from on deck, "All ashore who's going ashore!"

"Hey, that's me!" Jody exclaimed.

"Go on, then," said her mother, kissing her.

Jody hugged her back. "See you later."

"Have a nice day," said Gina. "And keep an eye out for dolphins!"

"You bet!" Jody said with a grin as she dashed away.

The dinghy was lowered into the water, and Harry rowed them the short distance to shore as *Dolphin Dreamer* sailed away out of the bay.

"What shall we do first?" asked Harry, once he'd made sure the dinghy was safely beached. "Go for a walk, take a nap, or have a swim?"

"Swim!" Sean and Jimmy shouted in unison.

"That sounds good to me," Brittany agreed, and Jody nodded.

Neither Brittany nor Jody was allowed to scuba dive without an adult partner, and the twins were too young to scuba dive at all. But they'd all been given new snorkeling equipment for Christmas. This was the first chance they'd had to try it out — and the clear, calm, shallow water looked like the perfect place to snorkel.

Jody glimpsed something large moving along near the bottom and dived down to see what it was.

Pale, sandy brown, with eight long, waving arms — it was an octopus!

It noticed Jody hovering close by and responded by spreading its tentacles as wide as it could and raising its head, making itself look bigger. It also turned a darker shade of brown.

Jody held very still. The octopus might attack if it felt threatened. Although it was only a small one, its parrotlike beak could inflict a nasty bite. After a few long minutes, the octopus seemed to shrink in size. Then it shot away, swimming rapidly until she lost sight of it.

Jody popped up to the surface just in time to hear Brittany shriek.

"What's wrong, honey?" Harry was at his daughter's side immediately.

Brittany's face was pale, and she was shuddering. "Some huge *thing* — it swooped at me. . . . I thought it was going to grab me up in its wings!"

Wings? In the water? Jody struggled to make sense of what Brittany was saying.

"Hey, there it is!" shouted Sean, pointing.

Jimmy added, "It's a giant manta ray!"

Now Jody saw it, too. She understood why Brittany was worried. The black-and-white fish was more than six yards wide and at least five yards long. It was flat, diamond-shaped, with two big "wings" that flapped gently to propel it through the water.

"Help! Get me out of here!" Brittany moaned, shuddering as the big fish swooped past them.

"Calm down, sweetheart," Harry said, holding her tight. His voice was firm and reassuring. "The manta ray is perfectly harmless. It's a plankton feeder. In fact, if you watch, I think you'll see that it's feeding now.

That's what it's doing as it loops through the water — it filters the plankton out of the water through its gills."

"Is it OK if we go closer and watch it feeding underwater?" asked Jimmy.

"You might scare it off if you go too close," warned Harry.

"Or it might sting you with that tail," said Brittany. She still looked wary, despite her father's explanation.

Sean laughed. "It's a manta, not a stingray!"

Brittany looked up at her father. "Do manta rays sting?"

"No, they don't," he said. "They don't bite, either — they're not aggressive at all."

"So can we go closer?" Jimmy asked again.

"Sure, go ahead," Harry replied.

Jody put her snorkel back in her mouth and followed after the twins. She was just as curious as they were about the manta, but she also wanted to keep an eye on them. The boys could be pretty boisterous, and she didn't want them frightening it away.

The manta didn't seem at all bothered as Jody and

her brothers swam closer. Just like Harry said, it was feeding, opening its mouth wide and then swooping around and around, sucking in the water and filtering it through its gills.

Jody was pleased to see Sean and Jimmy keeping a distance. They followed the manta ray but were careful not to make any sudden movements that might startle it. Their eyes were round with fascination as the huge, graceful creature swooped and glided through the water, grazing on its invisible food.

When Jody finally decided to swim away and see what else was going on in the underwater world of the bay, the two boys were still totally entranced by the manta.

February 12 — After lunch — Anaho Bay
If it weren't for the pesky little biting flies — they call them nao-naos here — this really would be paradise! The twins are running races until Harry says they can go back in the water. They say the nao-naos can't bite you if you keep moving, but after that huge picnic lunch, I am too stuffed to move!

I wish the spinners would come back — especially Twister. I would love to swim with him and get to know him better. I felt a real connection between us yesterday. . . . It reminded me of when I first met Apollo. . . .

Jody sighed and gazed wistfully into the distance as happy memories flooded her mind. Apollo was the first wild dolphin she'd met. He was a young bottle-nosed dolphin who lived in the waters along the south coast of Florida. A strong friendship had sprung up between them. He had saved Jody's life when she'd been knocked overboard during a storm. Later, she had helped him return to his dolphin group.

At last, Jody dragged herself back to the present and described the encounter with the manta ray.

I had seen pictures, but I had no idea how big they really are. Sean and Jimmy could hardly stop talking about it at lunch. They've even given it a name — Angel. That's because of its "wings," and the way it seems to fly through the water.

When their food had settled, they went in for another swim. They were just drying off in the sunshine when Jimmy spotted *Dolphin Dreamer* entering the bay.

As Harry rowed them back to the boat, Jody was surprised to see two strangers, a man and a woman, on deck. The woman was bronze-skinned and beautiful, with a large white flower tucked in her long black hair. The man had a round, friendly face and short curly brown hair. Even before he opened his mouth, Jody guessed the man was an American. Maybe it was the faded orange University of Texas T-shirt that gave him away.

Grinning broadly, Cam introduced them all as soon as they clambered up the ladder onto the deck. "This is Lewis Alberts — my best friend from high school. And this is his girlfriend, Monique. I couldn't believe my eyes when I saw him walking down the road toward me, thousands of miles from home!" Cam finished, shaking his head in amazement.

"I could say the same about you," the man retorted, his grin as wide as Cam's. "It's a small world, isn't it?

Call me Lew, please, all of you," he said, shaking hands with Harry.

"Anyway, I invited Lew and Monique to come aboard and have dinner with us," Cam went on. "Craig and Gina thought you'd be very interested to meet them, Jody."

Jody blinked in surprise. "Me? Why?"

"Well, you want to know more about dolphin-friendly fishing methods, don't you?" said Cam.

Jody nodded, still puzzled.

"Monique and I are professional divers," Lew explained. "Right now we're working with the tuna boat *Zelda*. It's our job to make sure no dolphins get hurt or killed in the nets."

4

"Oh, wow!" Jody exclaimed, gazing at Cam's old school friend. "Do you mean you help dolphins escape from the nets?"

"That's right." Lew nodded. "I'm one of *Zelda's* crew. *Zelda's* captain is Gus Franklin. He's the most responsible fishing-boat captain I've ever met. Among other things, he hires divers to make sure the dolphins can escape. Monique put us in touch with local divers, so it's not just me having to handle such a big job on my own."

"Is it a big job?" asked Brittany, sounding doubtful.

"The net is huge," Lew explained, turning to smile at

her. "It's almost a mile wide. And spinner and spotted dolphins like to travel in big groups so it's not uncommon to catch several hundred dolphins at a time."

Gina and Maddie emerged from the hatch just then, each carrying a tray.

"Cold drinks for our rescued castaways!" Maddie called out.

"Thanks, Maddie," Jody said gratefully, taking a glass of iced tea. "Mmm, mint!" She nibbled at the pungent green leaves, enjoying the fresh, sweet taste.

"That was a gift from Monique," said Maddie. "Isn't it delicious?"

Monique smiled. "It is traditional to bring flowers," she said. "But I thought you might like fresh herbs even more, after so many weeks out at sea."

"Mei Lin was thrilled," Craig put in, taking a drink from his wife. "And when dinner is served, I'm sure we'll all appreciate it."

"How about some mint tea for you, Cam?" asked Gina.

"That would be great!" Cam replied, accepting the glass she held out to him.

"We'd love to hear more about what makes a tuna boat dolphin-friendly," said Craig as everyone settled down on deck with their cool drinks.

"Well, there are various things that can be done," Lew replied, leaning back against the railing and making himself comfortable. "Gus Franklin still uses the encirclement method, which means that dolphins as well as tuna are rounded up in our nets, but he dips the nets deeper, so it's easier for the dolphins to escape. We also have safety panels and use a special fine mesh that a dolphin is less likely to get its fins or beak tangled up in."

"But don't the nets sometimes collapse, trapping the dolphins underwater?" Gina asked.

Jody leaned forward anxiously to hear Lew's reply.

He nodded slowly. "Yes, with such big nets there is the risk they might collapse. But there's a device called an ortza that is used to hook the nets onto the boat. If it looks as if the net will collapse, the captain can call for the ortza to be dropped. This drops the net, which releases the whole catch — tuna, dolphins, and all."

"Speaking of dolphins . . ." said Gina, gazing out to sea.

Jody turned to follow her mother's gaze. She caught her breath with excitement. "They've come back!" she cried at the sight of a big group of dolphins entering the bay.

"This is a dolphin bay," said Monique. At Gina's questioning look, she went on to explain, "There are certain bays all around the island where the dolphins come, day after day, to spend hours playing together."

Jody looked longingly out at the clear blue water where she had been swimming earlier today. Now, it was alive with splashing and the gentle creaks and whistles the dolphins made to communicate with one another.

Many of the dolphins were swimming along the surface of the water. Some were leaping into the air and spinning. Among those, Jody spotted one who seemed able to leap higher and spin around more times than any of the others, and her heart beat faster. Although he was too far away for her to see if there were any markings on his dorsal fin, she felt sure it was Twister. And, as she watched, he came leaping through the water, directly toward *Dolphin Dreamer.*

She leaned over the side. "Twister?"

In reply, the spinner dolphin launched himself into the air with a joyful chattering sound.

"It looks like you've made another friend, Jody!" her mother said with a warm chuckle.

"Can I swim with him?" Jody asked.

"If he doesn't mind," replied Gina. She smiled. "I think I'll join you. Just let me get my underwater camera."

"Us, too!" shouted Jimmy.

Jody turned to Brittany as her mother nodded in agreement. "How about you?"

Brittany hesitated, then shook her head. "No, I've had enough swimming for today. I'm kind of tired."

Jody didn't push it. Although she thought swimming with dolphins was just about the most wonderful thing in the world and would never pass up a chance, Brittany didn't feel the same. Brittany had made friends with some dolphins in a cetacean therapy center, but she still regarded wild dolphins with suspicion.

"How about you, sweetheart?" Gina asked, looking at Craig.

He shook his head with a rueful expression, holding up a half-empty glass. "Normally I would, but I'm a bit tired, too."

"I'll come with you," said Maddie. "Just give me a minute to change."

A few minutes later, Jody was diving off the side of the boat. Her body arced through the air and sliced cleanly through the water as she plunged in and began to swim. Soon she surfaced and looked around for Twister.

Here I go!

She didn't spot him right away. The dolphins she could see were all a short distance away and didn't seem especially interested in either the boat or the people who had come from it.

As she looked around, Jody saw her brothers nearby, talking to Maddie.

After she spotted her mother, Jody looked up at the *Dolphin Dreamer.* She was just in time to see a slim, dark-haired woman diving off the side.

A moment later, Monique came to the surface beside her. She smiled as she blinked water out of her eyes.

"Hi, Monique," Jody said a little shyly.

"Hello, Jody," said Monique. "I guess I'm like you. I can never resist the chance to swim with *te ariki o te moana.*"

"What does that mean?" Jody asked.

"It's one of our names for the dolphin," Monique explained. "It actually means 'the lord of the seas.' The local word for dolphin is *tapora.* But Polynesians like to give everything a descriptive name as well."

"Do you have any special dolphin friends?" Jody

asked hopefully. "Any that you've rescued from the tuna nets?"

Monique shook her head. "These are wild animals, Jody. I have helped many of them to escape, but I don't expect to change their attitudes toward people. Maybe some of them remember me and feel grateful — I don't know."

Jody felt a little disappointed by that. "Don't you think dolphins and people can be friends?"

Monique looked thoughtful. "I have heard of such friendships," she said slowly. "There are many stories of dolphins that have helped people who were in trouble. These things happen; no one knows why." Then she smiled. "But with your parents, you must know far more about dolphins than I do! I'm going to swim now." With that, she dived below the surface.

Jody was aware of someone swimming up behind her. She turned, expecting to see her mother or one of her brothers. Instead, to her surprise, she glimpsed a flash of dark gray skin, and a curving fin sliced through the water. Etched against the dark gray fin like a tattoo was the spiral mark.

With a soft *whoosh* of expelled air, Twister's head pushed through the surface. He gave Jody a sidelong look with one bright black eye.

Jody's heart beat hard with excitement. She resisted the urge to reach out and stroke Twister. Dolphins had very sensitive skin and sometimes enjoyed being petted. They often rubbed against each other to express affection. But she also knew that dolphins didn't like being grabbed. Human arms and legs, so different from the dolphin's smooth, solid shape, could seem like a threat, especially to a wild dolphin. So Jody kept her arms close to her body and waited to see what Twister would do.

The spinner dolphin swam around her in a circle, sinking deeper into the water. Then he leaped up, rotated his body once, and splashed down again, showering her with spray. While Jody was still sputtering, he did it again.

"What are you up to, Twister?" she gasped, wiping the water from her eyes.

"I think he's trying to show you how it's done, Jody!" Her mother's laughing voice came from nearby.

Jody turned to look at her. "Are you kidding?"

Gina shook her head, smiling broadly. "No, really. He's keeping it simple, just one spin. . . . That's how the parents teach their young ones!"

Jody looked at Twister, hovering in the water nearby. She wondered if her mother was right. Suddenly, she had an idea.

"I can't do it the way you do, but hang on a minute," she told him. She swam quickly back to the boat and clambered swiftly up the ladder.

"You didn't stay in long," her dad commented as she hit the deck.

"I'm not finished," she told him. "Just watch this."

Balancing on the railing, Jody cast her mind back to the high diving board at the public swimming pool back home in Florida and the long summer days when she and her best friend, Lindsay, would try to outdo each other with double and triple back and front flips. This wasn't quite so high and, unlike a diving board, there was no spring in the rail, but she figured she should be able to manage at least *one* good flip before hitting the water.

Holding her breath, and hoping Twister was watching, Jody leaped up and out . . . and *twisted* in the air, once, twice, before she splashed down. When she came up to the surface, she heard cheers from the twins and a scattering of applause from the boat.

But the response that meant the most to her was Twister's. She looked at the dolphin and saw him nodding and chattering loudly. There was no doubt about it — she had done the right thing!

Mei Lin had cooked an outstanding meal, helped by the wonderful flavors of Monique's herbs.

Crowded around the big table, everyone ate hungrily. At first there was little said, but gradually, as their stomachs began to fill and the level of food on the plates went down, there was more conversation.

Lew and Monique were curious to learn more about the Dolphin Universe project.

"Sounds like a great life." Lew grinned at Cam, giving his old friend a mock punch on the arm. "You lucky dog!"

"A good job on a fishing boat? It doesn't sound like

you've done so badly yourself," Cameron pointed out. "We've both ended up spending most of our time out at sea — just like we always wanted."

"How did you get involved in diving, Monique?" asked Gina.

"Oh, I could swim before I could walk," Monique replied with a smile. "In the old days it was taboo for women to travel in a canoe, so women *had* to swim. Of course, that was a very long time ago. But it meant there was a tradition of diving in these islands long before scuba gear was invented. So I guess it just seemed natural to me to become a diver."

"So you're part of *Zelda*'s crew?" Craig asked, passing her the wooden salad bowl.

"Oh, no." Monique shook her head and helped herself to some salad.

"*Zelda* has a full-time crew of nineteen," Lew explained. "I'm the only professional diver on board. The captain hires local divers on a part-time basis. Monique knows all the divers on Nuku Hiva, so we made contact with them through her," he finished, smiling fondly.

She smiled back and handed him the salad bowl. "You can meet the other divers tomorrow — if you're up early enough," she said to Jody.

"How?" Jody asked curiously.

"Monique and Lew are spending the night on board *Dolphin Dreamer*," Cam explained.

"Yeah, and our friends Jules and François are coming by in their boat first thing in the morning to pick us up," added Lew.

"We're going out cave diving," Monique explained.

"Do you mean underwater caves?" Jody asked, fascinated.

Monique nodded. "Yes, there are some wonderful sea caves around Nuku Hiva. I want to show Lew the Ekamako Cave."

Jody turned excitedly to her father. "Oh, Dad, can we go sometime before we leave?"

"Yes, please!" said Brittany. "I've never dived in a cave!"

"It's a very different sort of experience," Gina told her. "It's best to have a knowledgeable local guide. . . ."

"Like Monique," said Lew. "She knows the waters

around here like the back of her hand. Hey, why don't you guys all come with us?"

Jody and Brittany both turned their most pleading expressions on Gina.

But Gina was shaking her head. "I'm sorry — not tomorrow. Craig and I have already made arrangements to meet Dr. Serval. We're going to sail to Taiohae and spend the day there with him."

"Maybe Monique would take us all another time, later this week," said Craig.

Now it was Monique's turn to shake her head. "I would love to, of course," she said. "But the day after tomorrow it's back to work. . . . We won't have another day off for at least a week."

"And by that time we'll be gone. Oh, I can't believe it! It's not fair!" Brittany burst out angrily. "We haven't been able to dive for ages! What's the point of taking lessons and having all the equipment if I never get to use it?"

Jody bit her lip. She was disappointed, too, but she knew making a fuss was not a good idea. She looked anxiously at Harry, noticing his frown. Recently, father and daughter had been much closer. It would be awful if Brittany's outburst spoiled everything.

"Are Brittany and Jody qualified divers?" Lew asked.

"Yes," replied Gina. "But they're both very young; they still need experienced adults with them all the time."

"I used to work with young people at a dive camp in Florida," Lew said. "I'm a fully qualified instructor."

"And I teach in the dive school here," put in Monique. "I've often partnered with novice divers." She gazed at Gina. "All four of us are experienced divers. I know the cave area very well. It is not too deep, we have the right equipment, and we won't do anything dangerous." She paused. "So it will be quite safe for Jody and Brittany to come along without you."

Jody caught her breath with excitement. She saw Brittany's mouth drop open.

Neither dared speak. For a moment, everyone could have heard a pin drop.

Gina and Craig exchanged a long look, then looked at Harry.

"Would you like to go, honey?" Harry asked gruffly.

"Oh, Daddy, yes!" Brittany cried.

Jody looked anxiously at her mother.

Gina smiled back at her. "It's all right with us," she said.

Smiling happily, Jody turned to Monique and Lew. "Thank you!" she said. "I can't wait until tomorrow!"

5

February 13 — before sunrise — Anaho Bay
We're waiting for the other two divers to come pick us up. I've just eaten a bowl of cereal, and Brittany is still picking at hers. It's much too early to feel hungry, but Mom says it's important to have breakfast before going on a dive.

I am so excited about this! I've never been in a real cave before — especially not an underwater one! I wonder what kind of creatures live there.

"Do you have everything you need, Jody?" Lew's question made Jody look up from her diary.

She nodded, closing the book. "I'm all packed. I'll just put this away," she replied.

"I'm ready, too," said Brittany, getting up from the table.

"I think I can hear a motorboat," said Gina, coming out of the galley. She was carrying an insulated bag, which she gave to Jody. "There's some lunch here — should be enough for everybody," she said.

"Thanks, Mom," Jody said, giving her a kiss.

Gina put her arms around Jody and hugged her tightly. "Have fun, but be sensible, and pay attention to your partner," she said.

"Don't worry, Dr. McGrath," said Lew. "Monique is the best possible guide anyone could have to the caves around here."

"We'll take good care of the girls," Monique added.

The sound of a motor had been growing closer. Now they heard it idling just outside.

"They're here — let's go!" Brittany exclaimed.

They hurried up on deck and found that a motor

launch had drawn up alongside *Dolphin Dreamer.* In the motorboat were two young men who looked alike enough to be brothers, both wearing swimming trunks and brightly patterned shirts. They grinned, waved, and called out, "*Ia orana!* "

"*Ia orana!*" Lew called back. Then he explained to Jody and Brittany, "That's one of the local ways of saying, '*Bonjour.*'"

Brittany called back, "*Ia orana!* "

Feeling self-conscious, Jody tried replying the same way. "*Ia orana!* "

She was rewarded with even bigger smiles.

As they got settled on board, Monique introduced the two young men as Jules and François. She explained that they were brothers. "They don't speak English, but Lew and I can translate."

"I can if they stick to French," said Lew. "But the local language is beyond me."

The motorboat, with François at the wheel, pulled gently away from the anchored *Dolphin Dreamer* and began to head out of the bay to the open sea.

The sun was rising, touching the gray sky with

streaks of pink and gold. They traveled for a time in silence, enjoying the peaceful beauty of daybreak on the ocean and the smooth progress of the motorboat over the calm sea.

Then Jules brought out a thermos full of coffee and a bag of flaky croissants that he offered to everyone. Jody's mouth watered at the sight and smell of the fresh rolls. She was surprised to find that she was already hungry. The croissant tasted delicious.

As they ate, they talked about what they might see in the underwater caves.

"What I really want is a chance to get close to some hammerhead sharks," said Lew, dipping his croissant in his mug of coffee.

Jody stared at him, wondering if he was joking.

"You're kidding, right?" said Brittany nervously.

"I hope not," said Lew. "Monique promised me hammerheads and rays today."

"I can almost guarantee we'll see some hammerheads," Monique said. Then she looked at Jody and Brittany and gave them a sympathetic smile. "Don't look so worried! We won't get too close to them. There will be no danger."

"What about dolphins?" Jody asked. If there were dolphins around, she knew she wouldn't be worried about sharks.

But Monique shook her head. "Not inside the caves. Some of the tunnels are quite narrow, not the sort of place a dolphin would like."

The sky remained overcast as they traveled farther away from land. By the time they reached the dive site and François cut off the engine, rain was falling.

"It's OK, we can't get any wetter than we'll be underwater," Lew said. Then he frowned and cocked his head. "At least, I hope it's just going to be rain. . . . I'm not sure about that wind, though. What do you think, Mon?"

Monique gazed up at the darkening sky, looking unhappy. She said something in French, and a rapid discussion followed between her and the three men. Finally, although nobody looked pleased about it, they seemed to come to an agreement. François powered up the motor.

"Hey, what's happening?" asked Brittany, frowning. "I thought this was the dive site?"

"It is," said Lew with a sigh. "But there seems to be a storm brewing. It wouldn't be smart to dive during a storm."

"So are we just going to go back?" Brittany grumbled.

Lew shook his head. "No. We'll head for land, take shelter somewhere, and wait for the storm to pass. With any luck, it'll blow over quickly. We can come back out when it's calm and dive then. But we really don't want to be out at sea in a boat this size during a storm."

The rain was coming down harder now, and a wind kicked the sea into choppy waves.

Already soaked, Jody huddled into herself, trying to avoid the chilly wind.

"Ugh, I feel sick," muttered Brittany. "The way this boat keeps going up and down . . ."

"Try not to think about it," Jody advised. "Anyway, it shouldn't be too much longer now. We're not too far from land."

Even as she spoke, they were approaching a rocky

outcrop on the island's shore. François steered around it, bringing them into the calmer waters of an enclosed bay. He turned off the engine. The boat rocked gently in the sudden quiet.

But although the bay was sheltered from the wind and the rough open sea, it gave no protection from the rain, which was now lashing down, drenching them all.

Weathering the storm . . .

Jody gazed at the rocky cliffs that rose up all around, encircling them. She saw birds wheeling overhead, coming in to land on ledges and crevices in the cliff face. There was no beach — nothing but jagged rock formations on all sides.

"Aren't we going to land?" asked Brittany. "I thought we were looking for shelter." She pushed back her sopping-wet hair and blinked water out of her eyes.

"There's nowhere to land here," Monique pointed out. "And it's not safe to bring the boat too close to those cliffs."

"Anyway," said Lew, "even if we could land, you can see there's no shelter."

François said something then and pointed across the bay. Monique nodded. "Except for the cave," she said.

"Cave?" Jody repeated in surprise.

François and Jules began to check their air tanks.

"Are we going to dive here?" Lew asked, sounding puzzled.

Monique looked uncertain. "There is a cave here, as François said. You can see the mouth of it, just there."

Jody looked to where Monique was pointing. Sure enough, she could see a dark opening in the cliff face.

François said something she didn't understand.

"He says it's not safe to take the boat in," Monique went on, translating. "But we could go inside ourselves. That's what he and Jules are going to do. They've explored this area before. Most of the cave is flooded by the sea, but we could come up for air whenever we liked and still be protected from the wind and rain."

"That sounds great," Jody said, cheering up. "I feel like a drowned rat," she added, blinking against the rain. "Why is it so awful to be stuck out in the rain when it's so great to be underwater?"

"It won't be as exciting a dive as we'd hoped," Lew said. "No hammerheads, for one thing . . ."

"That's OK." Jody and Brittany spoke at exactly the same time, which made the others laugh.

"Never mind," said Monique, smiling. "You'll see your hammerheads another day, Lewis. This cave might seem a bit dull to you, but there will be lots of shellfish living there, maybe even some octopus."

"Let's do it," said Lew. He looked at Jody. "I'll be your partner, Jody, and Monique can partner Brittany."

"Great," said Brittany. She looked happy and excited now.

"We'll take our flashlights," said Monique. "And even though we won't be diving as deep as we'd planned, we'll still take all the usual safety precautions and stick together. It's important to do everything properly."

Looking at Brittany, she said, "Let's just run through our hand signals, to make sure we can understand one another underwater. Do you know what this means?" Monique made the hand signal that meant "Are you OK?"

Brittany nodded.

"How would you respond?" Monique asked.

Brittany made a signal back.

Monique nodded. "And if you're *not* OK?" she prompted.

Brittany clenched her fist and waved her forearm back and forth. "This, if I need help. Or if there's just some little problem, then I go like this," she went on, holding her hand flat and tilting it from side to side.

"*Très bien.*" Monique smiled her approval. "Now let's check our equipment."

Jody went through the usual predive check with her partner at the same time. No matter how unpleasant they all found it to be standing in the pouring rain on the small, rocking boat, and no matter how eager they were to dive, this was something she knew could never be skipped or rushed. They made sure all their air tanks were full and switched on, that all the hoses were properly connected, and that their masks were comfortably fitted.

Monique and Lew discussed the dive plan with Jules and François in French, then repeated it in English for Jody and Brittany.

Finally, they were all suited up and ready to dive.

Jules and François went over the side of the boat first in a backward roll. Monique and Brittany followed them, using the same method of entering the water. Jody and Lew went last.

Jody felt her insides fizz with excitement as she sank gently below the surface. She loved being underwater, loved the chance to see the world the way her beloved dolphins did. Despite her excitement, she was careful not to descend too fast and kept clearing her ears.

Due to the weather, visibility was not great, but it was easy enough to see the other divers. Jules and François, who led the way, took it slowly. Jody finned gently along behind Brittany, enjoying the peace of the underwater world after the wind and rain above.

Soon the mouth of the cave loomed ahead of them. The opening was even wider below the water than it was above the surface. All six of them could enter it at the same time. It was a bit gloomy — Jody noticed that Monique and Brittany had switched on their flashlights — but there was enough light filtering down from above to keep the cavern from being completely dark.

As she entered the cave, Jody looked around. The first thing she noticed was that they were not alone. She saw about a dozen large, dark shapes up ahead. Her stomach clenched anxiously as her thoughts flew to sharks.

Then two of the shapes moved out of the shadows. They began swimming toward the divers. One came into the beam of Monique's flashlight. As the shape became clear in the light, Jody's heart beat harder with excitement. It was a dolphin! Now she could see quite clearly that they were sharing the underwater space with a group of spinner dolphins.

6

Jody was very surprised to find dolphins inside a cave. She knew that dolphins — and especially spinners — didn't like confined spaces.

On the other hand, the entrance to this cave was so wide, and the cave itself was so big, that it didn't feel confining at all. It was easy to swim in and out with no worries about getting trapped.

But what had brought them here? she wondered. As the two dolphins swam closer, she saw that one had a squid in its mouth.

It was obviously freshly caught. *If there were lots of squid living in this cave, that might explain why the spinners came here*, Jody thought.

The one with the squid in its mouth swam past, but the other dolphin hovered in the water. It seemed curious about Jody.

Jody finned gently closer to the spinner and narrowed her eyes, studying its fin. It was Twister! Her heart gave a little thump of excitement.

For a long moment, the girl and the dolphin gazed at each other.

Jody felt thrilled and was moved by the trust he showed in coming so near. She wondered if she dared to stroke him, but decided it was better if she didn't. Friendships with dolphins couldn't be forced. It would have to be his decision.

Twister swam closer still. His eyes were bright and interested as he swam all the way around Jody. She wondered if he was surprised to find her so deep below the surface, and if he understood that she could stay underwater for a long time only because of the air tank she was wearing. When he poked his long, narrow snout into the air bubbles rising from her equipment, she was sure he had figured it out.

Just then, she noticed that Lew was coming toward her. In her excitement about meeting Twister, Jody had completely forgotten the rule about staying in constant touch with her diving partner.

Now, as Lew came near, Twister moved away.

Chatting with Twister

Jody longed to go after the spinner. But Lew was signaling to her: Was she OK?

She signaled back "OK," then pointed to Twister, then to herself, then back to Twister, trying to tell him that she wanted to follow the dolphin. She wished it wasn't so difficult to communicate underwater! The face mask and respirator made it hard even to read other people's expressions.

Lew must have understood — or maybe he just realized that Jody, like her parents, found dolphins more interesting than anything else in the world. He nodded. Then he pointed to himself and to her and clasped his hands together.

Jody knew he was reminding her they had to stay together. "OK," she signaled.

She looked around for Twister, hoping he hadn't been frightened off by Lew. He was hovering not far away. Jody looked at Lew and pointed toward the dolphin, indicating she wanted to go in that direction. Then she set off, with her partner at her side, heading toward the dolphin.

Twister had been floating gently in one place, as if

waiting for her, but as the two divers drew near, he suddenly moved, shooting almost straight up through the water toward the surface.

Jody stared after the dolphin in dismay. There was no way she could move as fast as that. But did Twister want her to follow him? Was this a dolphin game, or was he trying to get away from her? Jody's heart sank as she watched the dolphin disappear overhead. She had felt that some understanding, a tentative friendship, had been developing between her and Twister. Wild dolphins did sometimes like to swim and play with humans. But it was usually one to one. They didn't like to be outnumbered. She hoped that Lew hadn't frightened him off forever.

Lew touched Jody's arm and beckoned to her. She shook off her disappointment and followed him. Surely she would see Twister again. For now, there was this cave to explore.

They headed farther into the big cave toward Brittany and Monique. Jody could see that they both had their flashlights switched on and were using them to examine a crevice in the rock wall.

They hadn't quite reached the other two when Jody felt the water stirring as someone came swimming up on her other side. She turned her head, expecting Jules or François. But it was Twister!

The spinner dolphin glided smoothly alongside Jody, and this time he *did* come close enough to touch, bumping gently against her with the length of his body, the way dolphins did to each other.

Jody wanted to yell for joy. He had accepted her. They were friends!

Suddenly, she realized why he had shot away in the first place. Dolphins were air-breathers, like all mammals. Although they could stay underwater for anywhere between five and fifteen minutes, at the end of that time they had to surface to take another breath. Twister hadn't been frightened — he had just needed to breathe!

Twister slid swiftly beneath Jody and came up on her other side, rubbing gently against her. He watched her with one bright eye and seemed to smile.

Very gently, Jody reached out one hand and stroked his side. Her fingers seemed to slip across his amazingly smooth skin, so she pressed down more firmly. Then she had an idea and grasped hold of his dorsal fin.

Twister understood and glided swiftly ahead, pulling Jody along. Now she was moving more than twice as fast as she could have done on her own. It was a great ride!

As they drew near Brittany and Monique, Jody sensed that Twister was uneasy. She let go of his fin immediately and, sure enough, he veered off to one side, keeping well away from the other divers and from the wall.

Yet he didn't leave. He was wary, but not at all frightened. He continued to watch Jody and stayed closer to the divers than to the rest of the group of spinners, which had all moved away to another part of the big cave.

Monique and Brittany had found an eel lurking in a wall crevice. By holding her flashlight steady where the eel could see it, Monique lured the creature into poking its head out.

Jules attracted their attention by banging on his air

tank. When they all looked around, he pointed to the cave floor near his feet. At first, Jody couldn't see anything except the rippled surface of the sandy bottom. Then part of that surface moved, and she realized it was a ray.

This ray was not a giant manta; it was much smaller, although it had the same body shape. It was an eagle ray.

The ray rose from the bottom and hung there in the water, hovering a little way above the floor. Jules put out one gloved hand and stroked it gently. The ray rippled slightly in response, and Jules stroked it again. Jody watched, fascinated, wishing the twins could be here to see this.

The cave proved to be full of creatures, once you knew how to look for them. Some were hidden on the sandy bottom, while others lurked in the holes and crevices that riddled the stone walls. There were squid and octopus nestled in sheltering crevices, changing their color to blend in with the rock walls. There were loads of different shells, which looked dull and rocklike until you shined a light on them and discovered their surprising shapes and colors. There were also schools of small- to medium-sized fish darting every-where. Some of the fish made it no farther than the jaws of a hungry dolphin.

Jody tried to soak up every detail, to remember it so she could describe it later in her diary. This undersea world was Twister's habitat as much as the clear, open waters of Anaho Bay.

All too soon, Lew signaled to Jody that it was time to go up. She could see Monique making the same sign to Brittany.

They came up slowly and carefully, partners facing each other. Jody glanced up frequently, as she had been taught, to make sure there was nothing in the way. It seemed darker to her than it had been before, but maybe that was just because she wasn't used to coming up in a cave. Just as she broke through the surface, Jody inflated her buoyancy compensator to give herself support.

Out of the water, the first thing she noticed was the noise. A sort of booming roar filled the air, in addition to the echoing slap and spray of the sea. After the peaceful underwater world, it was a terrible racket.

And it seemed wrong somehow. Jody turned her face toward the light of the cave opening and saw what seemed to be a solid sheet of water.

"It looks like the weather's gotten worse since we went down," said Lew, his voice close to her ear. He sounded tense.

"It's a storm out there!" Brittany exclaimed. Her voice echoed spookily off the walls around them. She lowered her voice. "What are we going to do?"

She looked worried. Jody felt anxious, too.

Monique was speaking to the two brothers. Now she turned to the girls and switched to English. "We'll do just as we planned and stay here until the storm goes away," she said. She sounded very sure of herself, and Jody immediately felt better. Although the storm hadn't passed as quickly as they had hoped, surely it would be over soon.

"I agree," said Lew. "It would be too dangerous to go out to sea in a little boat in this weather. And there's no point in leaving a shelter like this one to sit in an open boat in the pouring rain."

Brittany frowned. "Our lunch is in that boat," she pointed out. "How long will we have to stay here?"

Monique shrugged. "Just until the weather eases up. There's no way of telling."

"Tropical storms usually pass quickly," Lew said.

Jody hoped he was right. She wished Brittany hadn't mentioned lunch. Suddenly, breakfast seemed a long time ago.

"Why don't we dive again?" suggested Brittany. "It's so much nicer underwater. As long as we have to stay in this cave, we might as well have fun."

Jody looked hopefully at Lew, but he was shaking his head.

"Sorry," he said. "I know it would be more fun, but we should save our air for the return to the boat."

"Yes, and anyway, you should have a rest before diving again," Monique added.

Brittany did not look pleased. "Some rest we're going to get in here," she muttered. "This place is terrible. It's noisy, the water's rough, and I'm getting cold."

Jody found herself agreeing with Brittany, but she

didn't want to say so. Grumbling and complaining would only make things seem worse. There was nothing they could do to change the weather. After all, they were dressed for the water, and their rocky shelter, wet and noisy as it was, was certainly better than being out in the wind and rain.

She looked around the big, echoing chamber, trying to think of something positive to say, and caught sight of a familiar, dark gray, streamlined body moving just below the water's surface. The long, slender beak of a spinner dolphin poked through first, and then the whole head popped up, only about a yard away from Jody. It was Twister. Then, all around him, there were small, explosive breathy sounds as the other spinners also came up for air.

All of a sudden, having to stay in the cave for a while didn't seem bad at all.

"Look, everybody!" Jody exclaimed, smiling happily. "The dolphins are still here!"

"Who cares?" Brittany said in a low voice. She scowled at Jody. "What difference does that make?"

Jody felt embarrassed, but she lifted her chin and responded, "It makes a difference to *me*."

Brittany laughed scornfully, but for Jody it was true. Having dolphins around — especially Twister — made her feel better.

She felt Monique's arm around her shoulders. "I agree with Jody," she said in her lilting accent. "To have *te ariki o te moana* on your side is very good news indeed."

Brittany snorted. "I don't see why! Unless a dolphin can change the weather so we can get out of this stupid place right now!"

François called out something to Monique just then, so she did not reply to Brittany. In her answer to François, Jody heard the word *tapora* and knew she must be telling her friend about the dolphin. Jules called something across to François, and the two brothers laughed.

"*Te ariki o te moana,*" Jody murmured softly as she watched Twister. *The lord of the seas.* It occurred to her that the Polynesians must have a very high regard for dolphins to give them a name like that.

"Jules!" shouted François, his voice echoing sharply.

Jody looked around. She saw that Jules was cleaning out his face mask. He looked up slowly, too slowly, just as a particularly large wave rocked into him. He flailed his arms wildly, trying to keep his balance, but it was too late. The powerful wave slammed him against the wall.

As Jody stared in horror, she saw Jules crack his head against a jutting rock.

No one was close enough to help or catch him.

His eyes rolled up in his head, and Jules slumped unconscious. A second later, he had slipped beneath the water.

7

Jody gasped as Jules sank out of sight.

Then she saw François duck beneath the waves and launch himself toward his brother.

A moment later, François had hauled Jules back to the surface.

Jody's heart was in her throat. Jules looked awful. His head was bleeding and his eyes were closed. He lay like a deadweight in his brother's arms.

Lew quickly paddled over to help François. "I've had first aid training," he said. "You support Jules, and I'll examine him." Then, remembering that François did not speak English, he gave instructions in his stumbling French.

"Oh, no," Brittany moaned in a high, trembling voice. "What are we going to do?"

"Hush," said Monique. She moved closer to Brittany, trying to calm her. "We will be quiet and wait for Lew to say what he thinks," she said, her voice soft but firm.

"He's unconscious, but he's breathing OK," Lew reported after a quick, low-voiced exchange with François. "I can't be sure about the bump on his head. It doesn't look too bad, but you never know with a concussion. We'll just have to wait for him to come around."

Lew didn't have to add that this would have been a much less worrying problem on dry land. Everyone understood that with one of their group injured they were all in trouble.

The minutes dragged by. Jules remained slumped in his brother's arms, unmoving.

Twister seemed as anxious as everyone else. At first, it was Jody he went to, giving a series of high-pitched clicks as he swam quickly around her. Then he stopped swimming and pressed against her legs.

Jody stroked Twister's sleek, smooth side. She felt comforted by the feel of his warm, solid body and the sound of his breathing as he inhaled and expelled air in little puffs from his blowhole.

"I'm OK," she told him. She didn't really expect him to understand her words, but it made her feel better to talk to him as if he could. "You don't have to worry about me. . . . It's Jules. He's hit his head, and we don't know what to do about it."

After a short while, Twister left Jody's side and swam in a slightly wider circle around Brittany. As Brittany stared at him distrustfully, the dolphin gave a stuttering series of clicks and then a long, high-pitched squeal.

He did the same thing to Monique, then to Lew.

"He's checking us all out," Jody said wonderingly. "I'll bet he's using sound in some way. . . . Dolphins learn about things by bouncing sound waves off them."

"That's ridiculous," Brittany snapped, her voice high with tension. "All anybody needs is a pair of *eyes* to see that Jules is the one who's hurt!"

As she spoke, Twister was circling François and

Jules. This time his inspection didn't end in a single squeal, but in a rapid, complex series of clicks and whistles. And this time the other dolphins responded to it. The cave echoed with their noise.

"Stop it!" Brittany shouted. "Stop it, or I'll scream!" Then she burst out crying.

"Hush!" Monique exclaimed. "*Cherie,* you'll make yourself ill!"

"Save your breath," Jody added. Brittany would be in no state to dive if she went on like this. "There's nothing to cry about," she finished.

Jody's remark at least caught Brittany's attention, although it didn't calm her.

"What do you mean, there's nothing to cry about?" Brittany demanded, choking back a sob as she glared at Jody. "Are you crazy? Jules is hurt and we're trapped here. How much worse do things have to get before you care?"

"We're not trapped," Monique said firmly. "We could leave anytime. We've just been waiting for the weather to clear . . . and now we're waiting for Jules to come around."

"And what if he doesn't?" asked Brittany, her voice rising nearly to a shriek. "We can't wait *forever*!"

Jody was about to argue, but Monique spoke first. "No, Brittany is right," she said. "We can't wait forever. We must get help for Jules."

Jody turned to look at the cave entrance. Rain was still pouring down outside. Then she noticed that Twister was swimming rapidly away, toward the opening. The other dolphins were all following his lead. She gasped and bit her lip, feeling a sudden pang of loss. How could Twister leave her now, when they were in trouble?

But maybe it was a sign, she thought. A sign that it was time for them to leave the cave, too.

Jody turned back to Monique. "How will we get Jules out?"

Monique shook her head. "It would be too dangerous to try to take an unconscious person through this rough sea. I wouldn't like to try it on our own. We need help."

"I'll go for help," offered Lew.

"No," said Monique. "You should stay here with François, to help him with Jules. I'll go."

"No!" With a sudden wail, Brittany launched herself at Monique, splashing all three of them. "Don't leave us!"

Jody sputtered and blinked water out of her eyes.

"I'm not leaving you," said Monique. "You girls will come with me."

"How?" Brittany asked, her voice wobbling.

"The same way we came in," Monique told her. "We'll dive and make our way underwater out of the cave and back to the boat."

"Will it be OK?" Jody asked uneasily. She couldn't help worrying about the dangers of surfacing in a rough sea, especially after seeing what a wave had done to Jules.

Brittany was silent, but it was clear from her face that she didn't like the idea very much.

"Of course," said Monique. "We must simply be very aware of what we are doing. Anyway, I don't think we have any choice," she went on. "We must get help for Jules."

"Hang on," said Lew. "You've never driven a boat before."

Monique bit her lip. "True . . . but I've watched you and Jules. And I can drive a car. How hard can it be?"

"That kind of depends. You have to think about the weather and how heavy the sea is," Lew replied. "And what if you flooded the engine? This sure isn't the best time for you to find out whether or not you can do it!"

François said something, and the discussion switched into French.

Unable to follow the conversation, Jody turned her attention back to Twister. She half expected him to have vanished into the open sea, but she was astonished to see that although they had left the cave, the group of dolphins had not gone far away.

Twister and six or seven other spinners were just outside the cave entrance, doing what their breed was best known for. They were leaping into the air and spinning again and again through the rain.

Jody caught her breath at the amazing sight.

As usual, Twister outdid all the other spinners. Most of the dolphins would perform three or four turns before diving down into the water again. But Twister made six or seven full-body turns every time he leaped.

Jody frowned, baffled. Why on earth were they doing this now? And why here?

She had always thought that spinners leaped and twirled out of high spirits. Dolphins were playful creatures, and spinners especially seemed to spend a lot of their time just leaping and diving for the sheer fun of it.

So why were they doing it now? And why right outside the cave's entrance?

Twister knew they were in trouble — Jody was convinced that he had sensed her anxiety about Jules and that he shared it. She didn't believe he could go from being worried to being joyful in just a few seconds. Dolphins were complex, intelligent creatures. There had to be a reason for what Twister and his friends were doing.

Did the dolphins think that putting on a show would distract the humans from their worries? Jody wondered. That seemed unlikely. She was sure that what the dolphins were doing was meant to help in some way; she just couldn't think of how. She looked around at the others and saw that no one else had even noticed what the dolphins were up to.

Lew spoke up. "So that's settled, then," he declared. "I'll take the girls back to the boat, and we'll go for help, while Monique stays here with François and Jules."

"I'm not diving without my partner!" Brittany exclaimed, a note of hysteria in her voice. "You can't make me! If Monique isn't going, neither am I!"

Lew and Monique exchanged a glance. Then Lew said, "Maybe it's better if I go alone. After all, you're all safe in here for the time being. If it weren't for the worry about Jules, we could all just wait for the storm to pass. But we can't risk that, with Jules unconscious. Somebody has to go for help," he finished firmly.

"Don't take any risks, Lewis," murmured Monique, her voice low and serious.

He nodded and smiled at her. "Don't worry. If the sea's too rough, or if there's any problem with the boat, I'll come back. I've got plenty of air for both trips."

"I'll come with you," Jody volunteered.

Lew shook his head. "Thanks, but no. François is going to need help looking after his brother."

Jody was about to argue, but she saw that Lew was looking at Monique and Brittany, rather than François and Jules, and she followed his gaze. Brittany was pale faced and miserable looking, with a glazed look to her eyes. Monique was speaking quietly to her, but Brittany hardly seemed to hear. Jody had an uneasy feeling. She knew she couldn't trust Brittany to stay calm. If she became hysterical, Monique really would have her hands full.

Jody's heart sank at the thought of a long wait in the cave, but she knew she couldn't abandon the others when she might be needed.

"I'll be as quick as I can," Lew promised them and began checking his equipment, getting ready to dive.

"Ahoy! Is there anyone in the cave?" a loud, Australian-sounding voice boomed from outside. And, although it had been masked until now by the sounds of the sea, there was the rumbling sound of an engine. Jody and Brittany stared wide-eyed at each another. Jody felt her heart lurch with hope.

"Yes!" Lew shouted back. "There are six of us — we need help!"

"Well, I'll be! How'd you get the dolphins to do that? Was that a coincidence, or what? They sure attracted our attention! Never seen anything like it! We only came closer to get some pictures of 'em," the man outside went on.

Lew and Monique exchanged baffled looks, while Jody grinned and hugged herself with excitement. There *had* been a reason behind the spinners' amazing performance just outside the cave! They had been trying to attract attention!

The voice continued, "We saw a boat at anchor with nobody on board, and no place to land — then we saw the dolphins were just in front of the mouth of the cave. They've gone now . . . afraid our boat coming so close must have scared 'em off. What's the problem? Run out of gas?"

"One of our party is injured — unconscious," Lew called back. "Everybody else is OK, but we need help to get him out."

"Hang on then, mate!" yelled the man outside. "The cavalry's arrived! Just tell us what you need!"

February 13 — bedtime — Taiohae
Twister and the other spinners saved us!

Lew and Monique and all the people on the boat thought it was a lucky coincidence, but I just know the dolphins did it on purpose! They must have noticed how much humans like to watch them perform and the way that boats will come close if they see dolphins leaping. We were all really lucky that a yacht happened to be passing by just when Twister and his friends began spinning outside the cave.

I'm sure everything would have worked out OK in the end, with Lew going for help as he'd planned, but it was such a relief not to have to stay in the water any longer.

The Australians on the yacht radioed ahead to the hospital in Taiohae to warn them about Jules. When we got into Taiohae Harbor, there was an ambulance waiting on the dock to take Jules — who was still unconscious — to the hospital. Dolphin Dreamer was in the harbor — Mom and Dad and Maddie were ashore with Dr. Serval — so there was no problem about me and Brittany getting home.

Mom and Dad said we'll stay here overnight so we can go see how Jules is first thing tomorrow.

I keep thinking about Twister and the amazing thing he and his friends did for us.

I wish there was something I could do for him, some special way of saying thank you. . . .

The next morning was breezy, bright, and sunny. Storm clouds from the day before had vanished like a bad dream. Right after breakfast, Lew arrived at the harbor in a small, battered red car to take them to see Jules in the hospital.

"There's no taxi service on the island, but luckily Monique knew somebody who lent me his car," he explained when the McGraths and Cam joined him. "Pile in. . . . I hope it's not too crowded! Luckily, we don't have far to go."

Jody got into the backseat with her parents, while Cam got into the front beside Lew.

"Hang on a minute," Jody said suddenly as Lew started the engine. "What about Brittany?"

"She's not coming," Gina told her. "She said she wasn't feeling well."

Now that she thought about it, Jody realized that Brittany had been unusually quiet and had hardly eaten any breakfast.

She shuddered. "Well, I hope whatever she's got isn't catching!"

"It's probably a delayed reaction to what happened yesterday," said Craig. "I'm kind of surprised to see you looking so bouncy, young lady," he went on, only half teasing. "Weren't you scared at all?"

Jody paused to think about it. "Yes, I was," she admitted. "But not totally. I was mostly worried about Jules. I was sure the rest of us would be OK if we didn't panic. And Twister being there made me feel better. Somehow, I just knew he'd look after me."

"You were right about that," said Gina. She put an arm around Jody and hugged her close.

They soon arrived at the hospital and went through

the glass doors into the reception area, where a smiling woman showed them to Jules's room.

Jody was relieved to see that Jules was awake. He had a bandage on his head and dark circles under his eyes, but otherwise he looked OK. François was sitting beside the bed, along with a large, majestic-looking woman in a loose, flower-print dress.

Visiting Jules with Mama Tahia

"This is Mama Tahia," Lew explained. "She is Jules and François's mother."

Mama Tahia nodded graciously at each of them in turn as she was introduced.

"We brought your friend some magazines," said Cam, handing a stack to Lew. "They're all in English, but he might enjoy the pictures. The twins put some of their comics in, and Dr. Taylor contributed one of his bird-watching magazines."

Jules's eyes lit up when Lew explained and showed him the magazines. He nodded enthusiastically, then winced.

His mother scolded him, then turned, still talking, and made a shooing motion at the visitors.

"Uh, she thinks we're disturbing him," Lew translated, looking sheepish. "She thinks we should go."

"Maybe she's right," said Gina. Setting down the rest of their gifts — a Dolphin Universe T-shirt, a big bar of chocolate, and a bottle of lemonade — they said a quick good-bye and left Jules in the care of his brother and mother.

"Will he be all right?" Jody couldn't help worrying as they walked away.

"Absolutely," Lew assured her. "They just want to keep him under observation for another twenty-four hours to make sure. And they've ruled out diving for another week or so."

Jody frowned anxiously. "So how will *Zelda* manage without him? Does that mean you'll wait until he's better before going out fishing?"

"No way!" said Lew. "We were supposed to work today, but plans changed. We're going out tomorrow, though — captain's orders."

"So you're one diver down," said Craig.

Lew shook his head gloomily. "Actually, it's worse than that. Two of the crew are down with food poisoning. So I'll have to fill in for one of them, which means I'll be driving one of the speedboats tomorrow instead of diving." He ran his fingers through his short, curly brown hair and sighed. "I've been asking all over, trying to find another experienced diver we could hire for one day, but no luck. I guess we'll just have to go out with only two divers — Monique and François — tomorrow and hope there aren't any problems."

Jody thought this sounded very risky. Surely the dolphins trapped in tuna nets needed all the help they could get! She wondered if *Zelda*'s captain could be talked into waiting another week. Then she had a better idea.

In fact, it was a positively brilliant idea. She had been wondering what she could do to say thank you to Twister and his friends, and now, all of a sudden, she saw a way.

"Lew," she said impulsively, "I can help you!"

"You can?" He looked surprised. "Do you know of some local diver I've missed?"

"No. I mean yes. I mean —" Jody paused and tapped herself lightly on the chest. "I can do it. I love dolphins, I want to help, and I'm an experienced diver — let me dive for you."

8

"Absolutely not!" Craig exclaimed, shaking his head and looking sternly at Jody.

"But why not?" Jody demanded. "I'm a good diver — and I know how to behave around dolphins. I could help guide dolphins out of the net. Please!"

"Jody, it's far too dangerous," Gina said gently.

Jody could hardly believe her mother was saying that. "Dolphins aren't dangerous!" she objected hotly.

"They can be when they panic," Lew added, "if they thrash about. Divers have been hurt before." He smiled at her sympathetically. "It's a really kind thought — and you *are* a good diver — but this is too risky." He shook his head. "Don't worry — we've still got two good divers."

"You could have three," Cam said suddenly. "If your captain is willing to take me on for the day."

They all stared at him in surprise.

"I didn't know you could dive, Cam," said Craig.

"I can't," Cam said. He grinned. "But I can drive a speedboat — and free up Lew to dive instead!"

An answering grin stretched across Lew's tanned face. He reached out and gripped Cam by the shoulder. "Hey, thanks, pal!"

"Don't mention it," Cam replied. Then he looked a little anxiously at Craig and Gina. "Of course, that's only if the bosses can do without me for the day."

"Of course we can," said Gina warmly. "We're not sailing tomorrow. We'll be spending the day anchored in Anaho Bay."

Jody was glad to know that Lew would be able to dive after all, but she was disappointed that she couldn't help, too.

"If you don't mind," said Lew, "before I take you back to your yacht, I'd like to find Captain Franklin and see if he'll agree to take Cam on as a temporary crew member. It shouldn't take too long. I have a pretty good idea of where we'll find him right now," he added, glancing at his watch.

"We're not in any hurry," said Gina.

"Yeah, we thought we'd be at the hospital for a little while longer," Craig added. "But Mama Tahia made it clear that Jules needed his rest."

They all got back into the little red car, and Lew drove down the bustling main street of Taiohae. After a short while, he turned onto a quiet side road that was lined with palm trees, flowering bushes, and small, well-kept houses. He began to drive more slowly. Finally, he pulled up outside a pink house shaded by glossy-leaved banana plants.

The house had a veranda on one side. As they walked toward it, Jody saw two men seated at a table there, playing checkers.

"Ahoy, Captain!" Lew called out.

One of the men turned to look at them and stood

up. He was a tall, strong-looking, dark-skinned man with graying hair. "Lewis? Is there some problem?" He spoke with a slow, southern drawl. His broad face wore a look of concern.

"No problem," Lew replied. "Just the opposite!"

He quickly introduced everyone to Gus Franklin, *Zelda*'s captain.

"This is Maurice," said the captain, introducing his friend. "He's the best checkers player on Nuku Hiva!"

Maurice laughed cheerfully and shook his head. He was a short, stout, elderly man. "May I offer you some refreshments?" he asked.

"No thanks," said Lew as the others shook their heads. "We're not staying. I just came by to tell the captain that we've got a volunteer to drive one of the speedboats tomorrow. If that's OK, I can work the diving detail instead."

"You're Lew's old high-school buddy, is that right, Cameron?" said Gus Franklin, eyeing him keenly. "I've heard a few stories about you!"

Cam flushed slightly as he laughed. "Well, sir, I hope Lew didn't tell you anything too bad!"

The captain chuckled. "Not at all! I'll be pleased to welcome you aboard first thing tomorrow morning. Hmmm, I don't suppose the rest of you have come along to volunteer your services as well?"

"Afraid not," Craig replied, smiling. "We have our own work to do."

"I'd like to help," Jody blurted out.

When Franklin turned his attention to her, she explained, "I hoped I could fill in for Jules, but Lew said diving into the net with trapped dolphins would be too risky."

"That's right," Captain Franklin replied in his deep voice. "I'm sure your parents wouldn't let you take such a risk. Neither would I."

"I know," Jody said wistfully. "I just really wish there was something I could do!"

The captain nodded slowly. "How's your eyesight?" he asked.

Jody was surprised by the question. "Pretty good," she replied.

"When we're at sea, she'll spot a dolphin before anybody else does," Cam put in.

"Is that so?" said the captain thoughtfully. "You're not afraid of heights, are you?"

Even more puzzled, Jody shook her head.

Captain Franklin looked at Craig and Gina. "How would you feel if I borrowed your daughter tomorrow? Of course, I might want to keep her for longer, but I'm sure you'll want her back."

"Jody could help?" Craig asked.

The captain nodded. "Pat Takita is my best spotter, and he's down with food poisoning at the moment. I used to do it myself, but I'm afraid that my eyes aren't what they used to be when I was younger. We need someone with good eyes to spot the dolphins. Of course, the best thing is if we can spot free-swimming tuna first. That way we don't have to worry about dolphins being caught in the nets, but that isn't always that easy. . . ."

"Oh, Mom, may I?" Jody asked excitedly.

Her parents exchanged a look. Then Craig grinned at Gus Franklin. "OK," he said. "We'll lend you our number one dolphin spotter. Just be sure to bring her back safely at the end of the day!"

February 14 — late morning — Nuku Hiva
Dr. Olivier Serval is on board with us and we've just left
Taiohae and are sailing around to Anaho Bay. Since Mom
and Dad need Maddie to help them, we have a day off
from our lessons today . . . and tomorrow, too! But Mad-
die has given me a big reading assignment, and some-
how or other I have to find the time to write a history
report. . . .

I'd completely forgotten that today is Valentine's Day —
until I logged on to get my e-mail and found a fabulous
electronic valentine from Lindsay! I e-mailed her back all
about Twister and the adventure we had yesterday and
apologized for forgetting to send her a card. I told her I
hadn't forgotten her, just Valentine's Day. Lindsay will
always be my best friend, no matter how many miles
separate us.

Well, I guess I'd better get to work now, since I won't
have time tomorrow.

Jody stowed away her diary in the locker beside her
bunk and got out her history textbook. She glanced
across the cabin to where Brittany was busy at her lap-

top computer. It had been a Christmas present from Brittany's mother. Jody had been almost as thrilled by it as Brittany, since it meant that she no longer had to share her own computer. Arguments over whose turn it was had been one of the worst things about living with Brittany. Life had definitely been easier since Christmas.

Still full of warm thoughts for her best friend far away in Florida, Jody made a resolution to be nicer to Brittany, starting now.

"Hey, Britt?" she said tentatively.

"What?" She didn't even look up from her screen.

"I just wondered . . . maybe I could ask Captain Franklin if you could come along on the *Zelda* with me and Cam?" She bit her lip, not certain she had the right to ask, yet feeling that Brittany would, like her, want to help the divers in some way.

Brittany shook her head. "Thanks, Jody," she said quietly. "But I'm going to stay here. Although I know I should try to do something to make it up to them, after being such a chicken in the cave. . . ."

"You weren't," said Jody, not very convincingly.

Brittany arched her eyebrows. "Oh, come on. I was totally, like: *buck-buck-buck . . . buh-gawk!*"

Brittany's chicken imitation made Jody laugh.

"Well, it could have happened to anyone," she said, chuckling. "I was scared, too."

"Maybe, but you didn't freak out. I totally freaked. And if we'd had to dive out of the cave . . . well, I couldn't have done it," Brittany said soberly. "I actually started thinking I could never dive again — it was just too dangerous. I talked to my dad about it last night," she went on. "You know what he told me?"

Jody shook her head.

"He said the sea *is* dangerous. It doesn't matter how good you are or how strong. The sea is just too big and powerful to be controlled. He said it was smart to be scared. He said *he* was scared sometimes, too, but that he faced up to his fear and did the best he could," Brittany finished.

"Wow," said Jody quietly.

Brittany nodded. "Until he told me that, I never realized you could work at being brave," she explained. "He said the important thing is to do your best, always, and not give up. I was scared to dive, so I need to dive again, to prove to myself I can do it. I asked your mom, and she said she'd take me on a dive tomorrow afternoon, here in the bay."

Jody felt a pang of envy — then a sudden rush of warmth for her mom, who was going out of her way to help Brittany.

"That's great," she said. "I'm sure you'll do fine."

"I hope so," said Brittany. Then she grimaced and rolled her eyes. "If I don't, I might as well just give up on diving and learn how to lay eggs instead!"

Jody was sitting on the forward deck with her history book — the assignment still only half read — when *Dolphin Dreamer* entered Anaho Bay.

"Hey, look, there's Angel!" shouted Jimmy as Cam and Harry began stowing the sails.

"He's been waiting for us!" Sean announced.

Gazing over the side, Jody thought it did seem as if the giant manta ray was gliding toward the yacht to welcome them back to the peaceful anchorage. She didn't know how her brothers could be so sure this was the same manta they'd befriended earlier, but decided it would be kinder not to point it out.

"Ask Mom if we can go swimming," Jimmy instructed his brother.

As Sean raced off in search of Gina, Jody quickly followed. Sitting out in the hot sun had made the idea of a plunge into the sea very attractive. She decided she would volunteer to keep an eye on the twins while they were in the water.

When she went into her cabin for her bathing suit, she told Brittany about her plan.

"I'll come, too," Brittany announced, shutting down her computer. "I've done enough work for one day. I need a break!"

"Great!" Jody replied. Then, remembering how frightened Brittany had been on first seeing the manta ray, she added, "The twins are thrilled because that giant manta is in the bay again."

Brittany's expression flickered with nervousness and Jody more than half expected her to back down. But then Brittany straightened her shoulders and tossed back her long blond hair. "Manta rays are harmless," she said, as if to reassure herself. "I saw a picture on a diving web site that showed a diver actually hitching a ride on one. Not that I'd ever do that," she added quickly, turning away to dig out her swimming things.

A few minutes later, they were all diving, or leaping, into the calm blue sea.

For once, Jimmy and Sean didn't let out their usual bloodcurdling screams as they entered the water. They were interested only in getting close to Angel.

The giant manta was a truly impressive fish, Jody thought. It glided silently through the clear water with a grace that seemed almost supernatural. Angel was like a gentle spirit from the deep who had decided to pay a brief visit to the surface.

Angel showed no alarm as the two boys swam closer, but Jody hung back with Brittany. She didn't want to risk crowding the manta and frightening it away, especially since the boys were being so careful.

As she watched, Jimmy and Sean swam closer to the giant ray. Jimmy's hand went out and gently stroked the broad black back. The ray remained where it was. Jimmy went on stroking it. After a moment, Sean paddled up beside his brother and he, too, began to stroke Angel's back.

For several minutes the ray rested near the surface of the water, letting Jimmy and Sean stroke its back. Occasionally, a little ripple would run through it, seemingly of pleasure, as it responded to their touch.

Eventually, Angel moved away. The two boys were af-

Sean and Jimmy bonding with Angel

ter it like a shot. Jody couldn't see how they did it, but they managed to find a handhold on that sleek, dark body, and as the giant manta picked up speed, gliding smoothly through the water, the twins were pulled swiftly along.

Then, suddenly, Angel dived. The boys hung on tight and went with it. Jody gasped and called their names. The manta ray swooped down and down, heading for the soft, sandy bottom of the bay. Jody watched anxiously, wondering if she should do something, as her brothers sank ever deeper underwater.

Long seconds passed. Finally, the boys let go and paddled frantically for the surface. When they burst out of the water a little later, they were gasping for air and laughing, but obviously thrilled by their wild ride with Angel. Like Jody and Twister, they had sailed halfway around the world to make a very special underwater friend.

9

February 15 — morning — aboard Zelda
I am up in the crow's nest, where I've got the most fabulous view! Nuku Hiva is shrinking in the distance, and the
wide blue ocean stretches all around. I feel like I'm floating in the sky!

I thought a crow's nest would be a little basket at the
top of the mast, and I'd have to climb a rope ladder to get
there. But that was a crow's nest in the olden days. This
one is a modern cabin at the top of a tower. It's kind of
like being in a lighthouse, with windows all around, or
even in the cockpit of an airplane. It's one of the boat's

control centers. Captain Franklin is here, too, with his computer, navigation charts, radar screen (the ship's radar system is searching for big schools of fish underwater all the time), shortwave radio, and on-board communication system. As soon as a group of dolphins is spotted, he will alert everyone on board to stand by. He can enter all the details into his computer, change the ship's course, and order the speedboats to be lowered or the nets to be made ready.

Jody looked up from her diary, feeling anxious that she might have missed something while she was writing. Although Gus Franklin had told her they were unlikely to find large schools of yellowfin tuna this close to shore, Jody couldn't wait to start dolphin-spotting. She put her diary away and picked up her binoculars. Carefully checking that the focus was right, Jody put them to her eyes and gazed out the window directly ahead. She scanned the waves for any signs of activity, then raised the glasses slowly to the sky, checking for birds. Then it was back to the sea again. This time, she turned slightly to her right, turning a little more each time until she was looking out the window directly opposite her first position. Then she gradually worked her way along the windows on the other side until she returned to the first, to start all over again.

Dolphins spend so much of their time underwater it was easy to miss one of their brief visits to the surface. Jody hoped she would be the first to make a sighting, but she had some competition. Besides the captain, who was monitoring the radar screen, two other crew members shared the job of scanning the surface of the ocean for signs of large groups of dolphins. These were a young American by the name of Marshall and a Marquesan man named Kae.

"Hey, Jody, you know about the clock system, right?" Marshall asked suddenly.

"You mean for locating the dolphins?" Jody said, lowering her binoculars for a moment. "Sure. We imagine we're standing in the middle of a big clock face, with twelve o'clock being at the front of the boat, and use the numbers to tell everybody where we've seen something."

Marshall nodded, staring fixedly through his binoculars in one direction. "So you'll know what I mean when I say, 'Rough water at three o'clock.'"

Immediately, everyone turned to look to the right. Even Captain Franklin picked up his binoculars, ignoring the radar and computer screens for once.

Jody found the patch of water Marshall had noticed. She stared intently, searching for something more. Yes, there was something just below the water there, churning it up. . . . Then she saw what looked like a little puff of smoke, and she caught her breath in surprise.

"That looks like a whale's blow!" she exclaimed.

"Yes," said Kae. "That is a whale."

Although it wasn't what they were looking for, Jody still felt excited and kept the binoculars focused on that spot, hoping to see more of the whale. However, she was unable to see anything more than the puff formed by its breathing, and that soon vanished in the distance.

The whale was the only excitement of the morning. Eventually, Lew and Cam came up to relieve Marshall and Kae. They brought sandwiches and a thermos of coffee for the captain.

"You can go with Marshall and Kae," Franklin told Jody. "They'll show you where lunch is being served."

Although she was hungry, Jody shook her head. "I'd rather stay here and keep looking," she replied.

Cam grinned and gave Lew a friendly punch in the arm. "What'd I tell you?" he demanded. Turning to Jody, he said, "I told him you'd never give up. So we brought you some sandwiches as well!"

Jody smiled gratefully. "Thanks, Cam!" she exclaimed. She took a bite of a cheese sandwich and then, still chewing, turned her attention back to the wide, empty sea.

She scanned for a few minutes in silence, then something caught her eye. She paused and went back. She adjusted the focus on her binoculars and looked again. Yes, there it was again, movement just above the waves, gleaming bodies rising and falling. "Dolphins!" she announced. "Spinners at ten o'clock."

As soon as Lew had confirmed Jody's sighting of a large group of dolphins, Captain Franklin switched on his microphone and gave the order to stand by to lower the speedboats.

"Yikes, that means I've got a job to do!" exclaimed Cam, dashing away.

"What happens now?" Jody wondered.

"The speedboats will go out and round up the dolphins and herd them toward *Zelda*," Lew explained. "Once they reach us, the net skiff will be dropped off the stern." He added, "A skiff is a heavy, open boat, and this one tows the net. It will move around in a big circle, setting the net around the dolphins and the tuna."

Jody frowned anxiously. "Is that when the divers go in to help the dolphins?"

Lew shook his head. "Not right away, no. What happens after the net has made a complete circle is that a cable pulls the net closed underwater — like an old-fashioned drawstring purse. It stays open at the top, which is hopefully where all the dolphins are. The tuna should be caught much farther down, inside the 'purse.' That's when we divers go in," he explained. "We make sure none of the dolphins is trapped underwater and that all of them can get out safely. At a certain point, Captain Franklin gives the order for *Zelda* to back up. The net gets pulled through the water and, eventually, pulled out from under the dolphins, which can swim away," he finished.

"You'll be able to see it all for yourself," Captain Franklin put in, turning away from his console to smile at Jody. "Up here you'll get a great view — the best seat in the house!" He nodded toward the window. "Look there, you can see the speedboats going out now."

Jody moved closer to the window and saw two small boats leaping across the water toward the distant group of dolphins. When she used the binoculars, she was able to recognize Cam at the wheel of one of them.

She bit her lip anxiously as she watched the speedboats racing toward the dolphins. They approached from different angles and worked rather like a couple of sheepdogs to herd the large groups of dolphins, with their accompanying shoal of tuna, toward the waiting boat. Although Jody knew that Cam and the other boat driver would never hurt the dolphins, she couldn't help worrying that these beautiful, friendly creatures would be frightened. She hated the idea of trapping dolphins, even if only for a little while. Even if they escaped from the nets, they could be injured or suffer from the stress of being captured. Jody wished there was a better way of catching tuna, some method that didn't involve dolphins at all.

The dolphins, chased by the two boats, were now heading straight for the *Zelda*. As she watched the spinners through her binoculars, Jody saw that it was a very large group — at least several hundred dolphins. One of the spinners caught her attention by leaping higher than any of the others. She was too far away to be certain, but she couldn't help wondering anxiously if it was Twister.

Suddenly, Jody knew she couldn't bear to stay up in the crow's nest, so high above what was happening in the water. If Twister was among that group, she needed to be close to him.

She turned to Captain Franklin. "Didn't you tell me that the crew in the speedboats helps to see that all the dolphins are OK?"

He nodded. "Yes. They herd them in the right direction to get out of the net. If they notice any particular dolphins in trouble, they direct the divers where to go to help." Captain Franklin looked thoughtful. "It would be very useful to have another pair of sharp eyes at water level. Perhaps you could go along with your friend Cameron and work from that boat?" he suggested, smiling at Jody.

Jody beamed at him gratefully. "Thanks! I'd like that very much."

A few minutes later, Jody was aboard the speedboat with Cam and Monique. Lew and François were in the other boat, heading for the far side of the huge net.

The hot sun beat down, making the water glitter with reflected light. As they approached the bobbing corks that marked the edge of the net, Cam shut off the engine. Jody caught her breath at the sight of so many dolphins clustered closely together.

There were both spotted and spinner dolphins in the net. But although they had been traveling together, now that they were trapped, Jody saw that they had separated into distinct groups, each with its own kind.

She could hear them calling to one another, and the clatters, clicks, and whistles sounded anxious.

Many of the spinners had formed a large circle. Females and younger dolphins were in the center, keeping fairly still, with just the tops of their heads out of the water to breathe. Meanwhile, the bigger males were swimming around them protectively.

Watching the way they looked out for one another and tried to keep the younger ones safe brought a lump to Jody's throat. As she scanned the water anxiously, she caught sight of a fin marked with that unmistakable spiral shape.

"Twister!" she gasped, feeling her heart lurch.

"Is that the dolphin that got help for you guys in the cave?" Cam asked.

Jody nodded. "Yes. He saved us, and now I've helped trap him," she said bitterly. Suddenly, she wished she'd never agreed to come along and help look for dolphins. Maybe, without her help, they'd have missed Twister's group. . . .

"They won't be trapped for long, Jody," Monique told her gently. "Twister is in the best position to get away when the back-down starts. And he's keeping the rest of his group calm while they wait."

"Sounds like one amazingly smart dolphin," Cam said admiringly, and Jody started to feel better.

"Yes, he *is* smart," she agreed. "But what about the others? The ones who aren't lucky enough to be in Twister's group?"

"Actually, I've noticed that a lot of dolphins seem to understand that the best thing they can do when they're caught is to wait quietly near the surface," said Monique. "I suppose they've been caught before, and remember what happened last time. It's the younger ones and the first-timers that thrash about and get into trouble," she went on. "Those are the ones that need our help." She adjusted her face mask. "Well, I'm ready to go," she announced.

"Good luck," Jody said.

Monique gave her the thumbs-up sign. Then she entered the water with a gentle backward roll. Jody knew that this way of diving caused the least disturbance to the water — the divers did everything they could to keep from adding to the stress felt by captured dolphins.

"There's something I don't understand," said Cam, shading his eyes as he gazed at the dolphins swimming in a slow circle.

Monique gets ready to roll!

143

"What's that?" asked Jody, still watching Monique make her descent.

"Well, I've seen how those guys can jump," Cam went on. "They can leap really high in the air, even the young ones. So why aren't they jumping now? The only thing keeping them trapped in that net is a line of corks, bobbing on the surface. They're barely a foot high. If the spinners want to get out, why don't they just hop over the cork line?"

"I don't know exactly," Jody admitted. "But they just won't. Dolphins can be trained to jump over things, but they never do it in the wild. I guess they have an instinct that stops them. They would never jump into a pen or a net — or any kind of enclosed space — but once they're inside, they won't jump out of it. It's as if they *can't* go anywhere unless they can swim right out."

"So that's why they put dolphin doors in the nets underwater," Cam said, nodding.

"Well, that's the idea," Jody said. She sighed and shook her head unhappily. "But dolphins don't like going *through* things, either. Mom told me that the scientific term for it is that they're 'object shy.' Dolphins

144

will often refuse to go through even very big open-ings — I guess it feels to them like they're swimming into a trap if they don't have plenty of open water all around them."

"Gosh, that's tough," Cam said sympathetically. Then he leaned forward, peering down into the water. "It looks like Monique is finding that out for herself right now."

Jody gazed down and saw what he meant. Although many of the dolphins were grouped together at the surface, others had obviously decided they would be safer in this strange situation if they stayed down be-low, well away from the boats. Monique had managed to guide several of these dolphins to a large, square opening in the net. But they didn't seem to understand that this was a way out. The dolphins would swim right up to the door, then abruptly turn aside. It was al-most as if there were an invisible force field keeping them in.

Jody groaned with frustration as she watched Monique's efforts. Even when the diver glided through the gap herself, none of the dolphins would follow her.

"Oh, if just one of them would go through, I'll bet the others would follow!" Jody exclaimed. She thought of Twister and the way he took the lead in his group. The four dolphins she was watching now didn't have Twister's boldness. None of them was a leader.

As she watched, Jody could see that Monique was being careful not to frighten the dolphins. She didn't try to force them through the door. But even though they weren't afraid of her, they didn't trust her enough to follow her through the opening.

Then Jody noticed something very strange. Normally, every scuba diver is accompanied by a trail of silvery bubbles. Yet Jody could not see any air bubbles above Monique.

Just then, Monique began to rise quickly toward the surface, dropping weights to speed her progress. As she broke through the surface just beside the boat, she spat out her mouthpiece and gasped, "I couldn't breathe! There's something wrong with my air line!"

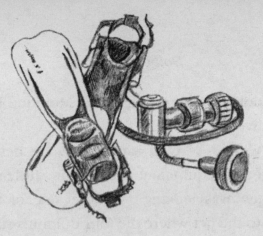

10

Cam and Jody helped Monique into the boat. She took off her air tank and began to examine the line. After a moment, she shook her head. "No sign of any blockage."

Cam was inspecting the regulator. "Here's the problem. Your regulator's busted."

"Can we fix it?" she asked him.

Cam shook his head slowly. "I don't see how. . . . You'll have to get a new one."

"But there's no time!" Jody burst out anxiously.

"Those dolphins need help *now*. Monique has to be able to dive!"

"Not with this," Cam said firmly. He held up the faulty piece of equipment and gave it a little shake.

Monique was looking over the side of the boat, down into the net where the four dolphins still lurked, too scared or confused to know how to escape.

"If those spinners don't come up into the back-down area before the captain winches the net up, they'll be caught along with the fish," she said grimly. "They need my help."

"There are two other divers out there," Cam pointed out. "Lew or François will have to do it."

"But they're too far away!" Jody protested, glancing across to the other side of the huge net enclosure. "They don't even know about these dolphins!"

Cam picked up the phone. "I'll call Mack — that's the driver of the other boat — and tell him to signal one of the divers to come over here."

Monique shook her head. "That would take too long. Anyway, I'm sure they've got their own problems on that side, other dolphins who need their help." As she spoke, she took off her buoyancy vest and lowered her oxygen tank onto the floor of the boat. "I'm going to have another try at moving those dolphins myself."

Jody stared in surprise.

"How?" asked Cam. "You don't have a spare regulator, do you?"

Monique laughed. "No," she said. "I'm going to dive the old-fashioned way, the way my people have done for centuries!"

Settling her face mask firmly over her eyes, the young woman drew a deep breath, filling her lungs with air, and dived over the side of the boat.

Jody leaned over to watch her swim rapidly down toward the tight cluster of frightened dolphins. Without her scuba-diving equipment, Monique could move more swiftly and easily. In fact, she looked as much at home in the water as the dolphins she was trying to help.

Monique swam around the dolphins in a tight circle, then sank below them. Moving up toward them, she waved her arms, gently shooing them. The dolphins moved upward, away from her. Jody held her breath. It looked as if Monique's plan to drive the dolphins up into the back-down area was working!

But after only a few seconds, the dolphins seemed to realize that Monique was no danger. She had startled them at first, so they had moved toward the surface. But now they broke formation and swam in four different directions, away from Monique, before coming together in another huddle. They were still inside the net, farther than ever from the dolphin door, and much too far below the safety of the back-down area.

Jody let out her breath in a disappointed whoosh just as Monique broke the surface, gulped more air, and dived down again.

Cam's phone suddenly trilled, startling them both.

"Yes?" he muttered. "Cameron Tucker here." He listened for a moment, then shook his head. "No, we're not ready for back-down. There are four dolphins still down in the net. Monique's trying to get them up into the back-down area. Three minutes? Yeah, hope so . . . Uh-huh, I understand that. I'll give you a buzz when we're OK." Cam looked worried as he closed the connection.

"What's wrong?" Jody asked.

"The rest of the net is clear of dolphins," he told her. "Captain wants to start the back-down."

"But you told him to wait for our dolphins — there's no problem with that, is there?" she asked.

Cam shrugged uneasily. "Well, you see, there's a bunch of dolphins that François and Lew only just managed to chase up into the back-down area," he explained. "Lew says they're really skittish. He's worried that if we wait too long, those dolphins might panic, dive down again, and get tangled up in the net or something. Then we'd have a really serious problem."

Jody bit her lip anxiously. The longer they had to wait, the more likely it was that more things would go wrong. She looked across the net area, the water heaving with the shining gray bodies of nervous or patient dolphins. She spotted Twister right away. He was circling protectively around a small group of dolphins, keeping them waiting calmly in the back-down area. The sight made Jody feel more hopeful. She looked down to see how Monique was doing.

The dark-haired woman was hovering in the water,

almost near enough to touch one of the four dolphins. She did not reach out or make any movement. After a long moment, Monique kicked with her fins and began to rise, still very slowly, toward the surface. She broke through and gasped, her chest heaving.

"Hey, look, I don't want to worry you, but we haven't got much time," Cam called to her. "Everybody else is ready to go. Lew's afraid that if we wait too long, some of the other dolphins are going to panic and get into worse trouble."

"I'm doing my best," Monique replied. "I'm trying to make them trust me, or at least feel curious. Then maybe they'll follow me to safety." Taking a deep breath, she dived down again.

"This isn't going to work," Cam muttered. He looked at Jody. "What do you think? You know about dolphins. How long does it take to make friends with one?"

Jody thought of Twister and how he'd seemed interested in her from the start. But she knew most spinners weren't like Twister. "It depends on the dolphin," she said.

"But it could take a long time, right?" said Cam.

Jody nodded unhappily.

"We need another diver," Cam decided, picking up the phone again. "We haven't got time for this — and Monique can't stay down there forever without air! I'll bet Lew and François could make them move."

Jody hung over the side, watching Monique approach the dolphins and willing her to be successful. Meanwhile, Cam spoke briefly on the phone. It didn't sound like he'd gotten the reply he'd expected.

"What's wrong?" she asked, looking around at him.

"The dolphins are edgy," he replied. "I wanted Mack to bring the boat around here, to let Lew and François dive, but he's afraid if he starts up the speedboat it could scare the dolphins near them. They might dive deeper into the net. We *have* to start backing up."

"Or get the captain to release the net," Jody reminded him.

Cam shook his head, grim-faced. "I wouldn't set your heart on his doing that, Jody."

Jody stared at him in disbelief, thinking of the kindly, courteous captain. "Cam, he will! He cares about dolphins!"

153

"He cares about his crew, too, and his business. Fishermen have to be practical. Every day he's out at sea costs money. A catch this big is worth a lot." Cam reached out to touch Jody's arm. "I think he might have to risk the lives of a few dolphins rather than the livelihoods of nineteen people."

Jody's stomach hurt. She had the terrible feeling that Cam was right. Gus Franklin *did* care about dolphins — but he had other pressures on him as well.

"Monique just needs a little more time," she said. "I'm sure she can do it. . . ." But she wasn't really sure at all. She wished she dared to dive over the side herself, since the other divers were so far away. It was obvious that Monique needed help to make the dolphins move.

"Time is just what we don't have," Cam pointed out. "The longer those four dolphins hang around down there, the more likely it is that others will get into trouble."

Suddenly, Jody heard some urgent clicking beside her. She looked around and saw Twister's friendly face poking out of the water. "Twister," she gasped. "Have you come to help?"

Twister flipped his tail and disappeared under the water, heading like an arrow toward the four spinner dolphins below him. Maybe he heard the anxious sounds they were making to one another and understood what was going on, Jody thought.

She could hear loud, rapid clicks and whistles coming from him as he charged into the group of nervous dolphins, slamming one broadside with his body.

Jody caught her breath with shock. She hadn't thought of her friendly, caring Twister as aggressive, but now he seemed determined to fight. Or maybe he just understood that they didn't have much time?

They scattered, but he was too quick for them, darting around to force them to stay in tight formation, then driving them, with nips and shoves, toward the surface.

Monique burst through the waves, gasping for air, but Jody hardly noticed, all her attention fixed on Twister and the dolphins he was chasing. In their need to get away from Twister, the four dolphins had forgotten all about their fear of the net and the boats. Now, for the moment at least, all the dolphins were safely within the back-down area.

Cam didn't waste any time. He gave the signal to the other boat at the same moment as he pressed the button on his phone to speed-dial the captain. "Ready to reverse," he said.

Jody helped Monique clamber back into the boat. Seconds later, the roar of *Zelda*'s engines filled the air, and the huge fishing boat began to back up, pulling the cork line below the surface.

As soon as their way was clear, the dolphins surged forward like a glittering tidal wave, with Twister at the head as usual. Those who were slower to react were caught by the pressure wave created by the boat's movement and washed out of the net, out to the open sea and safety.

Jody's throat was tight with emotion as she watched the dolphins leaping and swimming away as fast as they could. One of them spun higher and longer than the rest, his silver skin sparkling like a thousand diamonds in the sunlit spray. "Well done, Twister," Jody whispered, her eyes filling with happy tears. "And thank you."

Monique murmured something softly, in her own language. Jody recognized the phrase for dolphins, *te ariki o te moana,* and thought she understood: *The lords of the sea were safe in their kingdom.*

Twister and friends came to say good-bye . . .

February 19 — bedtime — Anaho Bay
Tomorrow we'll be heading out to sea again, beginning the next leg of our dolphin voyage.

I swam with Twister one last time today, and it was the best ever. Did he know I was saying good-bye when I hugged him just before I climbed back on board?

We had dinner on deck so we could watch the hundreds of spinner dolphins dancing and playing in the waters of Anaho Bay as the sun went down. Such an unforgettable sight. Mom got some of it on video, and I took a few photos myself, but nothing can match the reality.

Twister stayed behind when all the other spinners began to leave the bay. I played my recorder to him, and he whistled back to me, then he leaped and spun in the last rays of the setting sun — I counted nine full-body turns! — before he went off to join the others in the open sea.

Twister — te ariki o te moana — I'll never forget you. You really are the lord of the sea.